"What about the sur[...] asked.

"Totally forgot." Monte glanced about. "Where'd you two put it?"

Luna whispered, "Somewhere secret." She looked at Evie. "Close your eyes."

Evie complied, her smile expanding at the sound of little feet scurrying across the carpet. She heard Callie's instructions to open her eyes on the count of three.

She did, laughing at their "Surprise." The twins gave over a basket filled with snowflakes cut from paper, hand-drawn pictures, slices of gum and a few other random items. They must have scoured the house in search of "treasures" to give her.

How precious.

"Do you like it?" Callie bounced on the balls of her feet.

"I absolutely love it." Evie's gaze shot to Monte, and her breath caught to find him watching her with an intensity that turned her insides to jelly.

That was yet another reason she was grateful she'd soon be away from this ranch—and this much-too-handsome cowboy.

The longer she stayed, the less likely she'd leave with her heart intact.

Jennifer Slattery is a writer and speaker who has addressed women's and church groups across the nation. As the founder of Wholly Loved Ministries, she and her team help women rest in their true worth and live with maximum impact. When not writing, Jennifer loves spending time with her adult daughter and hilarious husband. Visit her online at jenniferslatterylivesoutloud.com to learn more or to book her for your next women's event.

Books by Jennifer Slattery

Love Inspired

Restoring Her Faith
Hometown Healing
Building a Family
Chasing Her Dream
Her Small-Town Refuge

Sage Creek

Falling for the Family Next Door
Recapturing Her Heart
Christmas on the Ranch

Visit the Author Profile page at LoveInspired.com.

Christmas
on the Ranch

JENNIFER SLATTERY

LOVE INSPIRED
INSPIRATIONAL ROMANCE

LOVE INSPIRED®
INSPIRATIONAL ROMANCE

Recycling programs
for this product may
not exist in your area.

ISBN-13: 978-1-335-93693-6

Christmas on the Ranch

Copyright © 2024 by Jennifer Slattery

Love Inspired
22 Adelaide St. West, 41st Floor
Toronto, Ontario M5H 4E3, Canada
www.LoveInspired.com

Printed in Lithuania

MIX
Paper | Supporting
responsible forestry
FSC® C021394

For we that are in this tabernacle do groan, being burdened: not for that we would be unclothed, but clothed upon, that mortality might be swallowed up of life.

—*2 Corinthians* 5:4

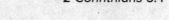

Dedicated to my sister and friend, Jesseca Randall,
who showed up for me during some of
my hardest moments.

Chapter One

Following her phone's GPS down a long, two-lane highway, Evie Bell slowed as she neared the wooden archway of Bowman's Rough Stock Ranch.

New Day Caregivers hadn't been joking when they'd referred to her assignment location as "off-the-beaten path." She'd expected country lodging but assumed she'd at least be near a shopping mall or steakhouse. Her brief drive down Main Street had dashed all hopes of weekend entertainment. Sage Creek, Texas, boasted little more than an old-fashioned diner, a coffeehouse/bookstore, a library and a handful of boutiques.

Decorated for Christmas, the town itself was beautiful. But she still had to wonder, what did the locals do for fun? Horse riding and hunting?

She'd hired on as a traveling in-home caregiver, hoping to blend her love for people with her passion for adventure.

She'd anticipated diverse backgrounds and cultures and exploration of new locations during her off hours. She had *not* expected to land in horse country, as Sage Creek's welcome sign had so proudly proclaimed. Until now, she'd turned down rural assignments. But this one came with a significant financial bonus.

She feared this assignment would be her loneliest yet.

At least she'd only be here three weeks, during which time she hoped to earn enough favor with her boss to secure the next big-city assignment. Then she'd enroll in nursing school, which would widen her options and increase her salary.

Maybe she could even work at a local hospital. *"And meet a handsome and available doctor?"* She laughed as her mom's teasing words replayed through her mind. But the statement did carry some truth. The closer she came to thirty, the louder her biological clock ticked. She was ready to find a life partner, to build a family.

Dust kicked up behind her as she drove toward the sound of bellowing cattle. As she passed pastures bisected by a fence and stables, two large barking dogs raced after her. She sucked in a breath, her gaze shooting from them to the handful of cowboys talking outside an arena. She assumed one of them was Monte Bowman, the ranch owner and the man responsible for her being here.

She sensed this was going to be far from a spa experience.

What had she gotten herself into?

She mentally reviewed the details from her client's file. Monte was a single father in his late twenties, raising twin five-year-old girls. His great-aunt, age seventy-five, had stage 3C ovarian cancer.

The aunt and kids, Evie could handle. But if the guy was expecting her to do any type of ranching, he was in for a disappointment. New Day Caregivers wasn't paying her enough for that.

She followed the curve of the road past more grassland bordered by mature trees to a blue single-story with a timber-frame portico. The covered porch bore simple fir garlands woven through the railings and accented every couple feet with red bows. Two vibrant poinsettias burst from pots wrapped in gold paper and were positioned on either side of the front door.

She wasn't surprised by their lack of lights. Monte had probably struggled to manage his family, let alone worry about decorations. Although she did find it odd that Tracy, their former caregiver, hadn't made the place more festive.

Maybe that would be a way she could connect with the Bowman children. She could make hot cocoa, turn on holiday music and invite them to adorn their Christmas tree with ornaments and tinsel.

She parked behind a maroon four-door with a large smiley-face sticker in its back window. A red pickup sat in the shade of a large gray shed a few feet away. The dogs, one with long black fur and pointed ears, the other splotched with three shades of brown, yapped near her door, as if daring her to step outside. Hopefully, someone would hear them and come out of the house to escort her in.

Until then, she'd stay put.

She shot Mr. Bowman and his great-aunt a text to let them know she'd arrived—in case they hadn't gathered as much from all the ruckus—and pulled her makeup bag from her purse.

When she was young, her dad used to make a game of counting the freckles on her face. "Sun kisses", he called them. Said she got her auburn hair and porcelain skin from her mom, her silver-blue eyes from him, and her quiet nature from the good Lord above.

A tap on her side window startled her, and she turned to see a broad-chested man with light brown eyes rimmed in green peering at her from beneath a gray cowboy hat, espresso-colored hair curling up under the brim.

With his strong jaw, thick brows and slight smile, he looked like he belonged on the cover of a clothing catalog.

Donning a professional smile despite an unexpected flutter through her midsection, she lowered her window. "Hello. I'm Evie Bell." She handed him her business card.

"Figured as much." He tipped his hat at her. "I'm Monte Bowman. Martha, your patient, is my great-aunt."

"Nice to meet you." They'd spoken briefly by phone a few days ago.

He opened her door for her. "Welcome to what most folks around here refer to as horse country."

Her gaze shot past him to the dogs, seated on either side of him, ears alert, eyes trained on her.

"Don't let these loudmouths fool you none." He flicked a hand toward the larger of the two. "They're a pair of biteless beasts." He chuckled. "The black one's named Max. He's as big of a baby as they come. This other guy's Finn, and he likes to think he runs the place and single-handedly keeps our fifteen-hundred-pound bulls in check."

She glanced at the animals grazing in the nearest field. "Wow. They're massive."

"About half a truck."

She eyed the fence. It didn't look as robust as she'd like, considering all the muscle contained inside. "They ever get out?"

He gave a slight shrug. "Once in a while, if a corner post gets knocked down."

Not the most encouraging response he could've given. She was quickly regretting accepting this assignment.

"Come on in." He motioned her forward. "Let me introduce you to my aunt and girls."

She grabbed her purse from the floorboard. "That sounds great."

He climbed the steps and paused on the stoop. "Excuse the mess. If my aunt was feeling better, there wouldn't be a dish out of place. But you know how it is."

"I understand completely, and I hope I can alleviate some of your stress." People tended to crave order more when their lives felt chaotic. Experience had taught her that. Tidying up their living spaces was one of the easiest ways she could increase their peace.

Opening the front door, he indicated for her to precede

him. He smelled like an enticing mixture of leather, cedar and citrus.

Once inside, he took her coat and hung it up for her. "Weatherman's predicting high sixties next week. I'd say that's one of the blessings of hill country winters. My girls would disagree. They're always hankering for a white Christmas."

"I'm with them. Snow always makes things seem more festive. But then again, I don't spend nearly as much time in the elements as you do." She hoped he wouldn't expect her to take on outside chores.

He moved a pile of children's clothes and a well-loved blanket to clear space on the brown leather couch. "Have a seat."

Coloring pages, pencils, crayons and partially eaten bags of crackers cluttered the coffee table. A mound of shoes gathered near the door, and dust danced in the sunbeams slanting through the window. A fake-looking tree stood in the corner. The sporadic and low placement of ornaments indicated the children had helped.

Although the home was slightly disheveled, it was cleaner than she'd expected, all things considered.

Monte looked from the empty kitchen that extended from the den to a back hall. "I'll go see where the ladyfolk are."

Nodding, she set her purse at her feet and sat with her back straight, ankles crossed, fingers intertwined over her knees. These initial encounters always felt like job interviews, this one even more so, considering the termination of their previous caretaker.

He returned. "My aunt's catching a nap. Lucy Carr, a family friend from church, must've taken the girls to their tree house. Can I get you something to drink? Cup of coffee, sweet tea or iced lemonade?"

"Whatever's easiest, thank you."

He nodded and retreated into the kitchen. The sound of

a cupboard door then fridge opening and closing followed. "Supper's in a couple hours."

"Can I help with that?"

"I'll just pull out some leftovers. The local quilting club brought us enough food to about feed half of Sage Creek."

"That's thoughtful."

He returned with two tall, steaming mugs and handed her one. "You okay with hot chocolate?"

She inhaled the rich, soothing scent. "That sounds lovely."

He sat kitty-corner to her. "Figured you might want something to help fight off the chill. As to our church family, not sure what we would've done without them." His expression tightened. "You heard what happened with Ms. Tracy Gray, the gal you're replacing?"

"I know she was let go."

"I came home from a rodeo to find her gone, my aunt sleeping, and the girls running amuck."

"That must've felt like a betrayal."

"She said that was just the once." He scoffed. "I'm just glad my Callie—she's the risk-taker of the two—didn't get caught between a fence railing and a fifteen-hundred-pound bull."

Evie could tell he didn't trust her. Why should he, considering what had happened with the last caregiver? He'd had plenty cause to sever his contract. The fact that he hadn't showed how much he needed help.

He studied her for a moment. "I 'spect your outfit gave you the rundown on my great-aunt. She'll turn seventy-six this February, and this is her second bout with cancer. They say that makes it harder to fight, but if anyone can beat this monster, she can. She's one tough lady. Proud, too, which means she might not ask for help when she needs it or speak up when she's in pain."

"I'll keep that in mind."

"Bonus points if you can make her laugh. She especially loves it when the girls put on shows for her."

That had to be hilarious and adorable. "Does she have children?"

He shook his head. "Never married. Always said she got her kid-fix working for the school system. Taught sixth grade for nearly four decades. When my ex-wife, now deceased, left us three and a half years ago, she moved in to help me raise them."

Left as in died? Except the way he frowned when he spoke suggested she'd taken off before her death.

"I can't imagine how challenging that must have been, running this ranch as a single dad." Then to have his great-aunt get sick? Poor guy probably felt like life had kneed him in the chest then hurled him in white water rapids without a vest.

Considering his good looks, she was surprised some pretty woman hadn't pranced into his world already. Did the fact that he was single mean he had commitment issues?

That wasn't any of her business.

"Aunt Martha was a godsend." He rubbed the back of his neck. "As you can imagine, she means the world to my girls. And they do a great job of keeping her entertained." He chuckled.

"I look forward to meeting them." She took a sip of her drink, her gaze drifting to a series of photos displayed on the far wall. In one of them, he stood beside two brunette toddlers sitting on a spotted horse. "They're twins, right?"

"Yep. Turned five this past September. Two days shy of the kindergarten cutoff."

"Are they in preschool?"

"Start next week. I was late getting the girls signed up. When I finally did, they put us on a waiting list. They're good kids, but they're a handful. 'Specially Callie. That girl's always climbing up something, and she's got two gears—full speed

ahead, or stop. Whether she's running her legs or her mouth."
Fatherly humor lit his eyes.

She laughed. "Sounds like she'll keep me on my toes."

"That's a fact." He lined three crayons lying on the table
side by side. "You have much experience with children?"

His pointed expression revealed his concern. "Some." Only
not as a caregiver. She'd primarily worked with dementia cli-
ents, although telling him that wouldn't increase his confidence in her.

Good thing all parties had signed the personal care agree-
ment, because if this had been a job interview, she felt certain
the man would escort her out.

While she didn't fault him his apprehension, she needed to
demonstrate her competency before his last threads of trust
in the company shred completely.

She'd already spent her recent bonus—the incentive for
taking this job—on car repairs.

"Figure we've spent enough time chitchatting." Taking
their mugs, Monte stood. "Up for a brief tour of the property?
Thought you may want to stretch your legs some. Course, if
you'd rather take a moment to unwind…"

"A walk sounds lovely, thank you." She grabbed her purse, a
shiny purple bag decorated with iridescent beads that matched
her shoes, and stood.

He retrieved her jacket, which carried a slight floral scent,
from the closet and handed it over.

Her wavy hair, streaked with hints of blonde, reached just
below her chin and flecks of silver shimmered in her blue
eyes like an early morning frost. Standing, the top of her head
reaching his shoulders, she looked fit but not all that strong.
Her clothing was better suited for the city than a ranch. At
least she wasn't wearing heels.

He hadn't expected her to be so beautiful. Not that it mattered. He was much too busy raising world champion bulls, God willing, to fall for a gal that'd be gone quicker than a drought could turn pasture to dust.

Besides, he'd fallen for a city girl once, and was left with a heartache that took two years to bounce back from. And his girls were left with a gaping mama-hole.

Was Evie's attire evidence of her trying to leave a good first impression, or was she that ignorant about ranch life?

He'd find out soon enough.

She waited in the entryway while he wrote a note telling Lucy and Aunt Martha whom the car out front belonged to and where he was taking Evie. He figured they'd assume the part about the vehicle but might wonder where they'd taken off to. After depositing their mugs in the dishwasher, he poked his head in the fridge to note supper options.

Lucy probably would pop the casserole she'd brought over into the oven before she left, and they still had plenty of pickled beets and fresh tomatoes from lunch.

He loved knowing his girls would grow up in such a loving community, with fresh air, land to explore, and the satisfaction that came from working with their hands. That made all the struggles and setbacks he'd experienced raising bucking bulls worth it.

So long as he earned enough to pay the bills—a constant concern for any cattleman, those raising animal athletes especially.

That reality had caused his ex-wife deep frustration.

This ranch hadn't been enough for her. *He* hadn't been enough for her. So, when a wealthy horse breeder from Dallas started paying her attention, she'd bailed on Monte and her daughters. She was killed in a car accident a year later. He probably shouldn't have grieved her like he had, considering how she'd betrayed him.

Unfortunately, his heart had taken a while to catch up with his head.

Shaking off the thought, he turned and strode back through the living room to where Evie waited.

He opened then held the door. "After you."

She smiled then stepped onto the porch and down the stairs. Max, his ten-year-old Lab-mix, trotted ahead of them, tail wagging, while Finn, his younger buddy, chased after a squirrel scampering up a nearby fence post.

Evie fell into step beside him on the gravel road that led to the barn and stables, alerting him to her soft lavender scent.

She gazed toward the east pasture where about half his herd grazed. "How much land do you own?"

"Two hundred fifty acres."

She raised her eyebrows. "That's a lot."

He shrugged. "Might sound like it, but the average cattle ranch in Texas is near double that."

"Wow."

"Big animals need a lot of forage." He picked up a stick, waved it at Max, then tossed it a good twenty yards ahead. "I have seventy-five head of cattle. Thirty bucking-bred, twenty-five yearlings, three champion sires, twelve PBR" –she probably didn't know what that meant. "Professional Bull Riders, Inc. competitors, and the rest heading that way. Then there's half a dozen chickens, five horses, a donkey and two pigs."

"Your ranch's name, Rough Stock, is there a story behind it?"

He cast her a sideways glance. "You asking how I got started in this business?"

"That, and why you call it that."

He frowned. "Rough Stock?"

She nodded.

She was even greener than her city-gal getup implied. "That's what they call bucking broncs and bulls—like those cowboys ride in rodeos."

"Is that where you sell them, then?"

"Some. For others, I form partnerships with investors. They buy in for a thousand, I raise and train the bulls until they're old enough to compete. Then, based on how they do, we decide whether to keep them or auction them off."

"They get paid on their performance?"

He nodded. "My investors and I split the winnings. Not every bull's a champion, obviously. But if you get yourself a superstar, they can bring in hundreds of thousands of dollars."

"I had no idea. Or that they could be trained for that matter. Ever have a dud?"

"For sure. Sometimes, you'll get one that refuses to buck or won't calm down in the bucking chute. Got to auction them off, at a loss. It takes a lot of money to raise competition bulls. Ever spent time on a ranch, Evie?"

She shook her head.

Max trotted back and dropped his stick at Monte's feet.

He threw it again, farther this time. "This can be a dangerous place for greenhorns."

Running a hand up and down the back of her arm, she looked away.

A few months ago, he was convinced New Day Caregivers was the best outfit to care for his aunt. They'd asked him pages of questions, related to everything from medical needs to family preferences. They promised to pair the Bowmans with the best possible match, and in many ways they had—with Ms. Gray.

Until she turned irresponsible.

Seemed, when it came to Evie, the decision-makers had sent the next available body. Then again, he doubted they'd had much choice. Ms. Gray's negligence had left everyone scrambling. Regardless, he didn't have many options. As much as he loved Sage Creek, he doubted the town was high on caregivers' must-visit list.

And that was why Evie was here, filling in until her company sent a longer-term replacement.

Lord, we need You. Give Aunt Martha strength to fight this, keep the girls safe, and help me be the father they need without neglecting the ranch.

Because if his bulls didn't perform well, he stood to lose a lot more than his dream of raising PBR champions. Keeping this place in the black and paying for the level of care Aunt Martha and the girls deserved didn't come cheap.

He should be grateful Evie had come on such short notice, so close to Christmas, and to an environment that clearly made her uncomfortable. Poor woman's face had paled a full degree when he answered her question about the bulls ever getting past the fence.

Under other circumstances, her vulnerability probably would've triggered his protective side. To an extent, it did. And her delicate beauty stirred a reaction he might otherwise welcome. If she wouldn't be gone before his neighbor started planting his spinach seeds.

Regardless, he'd hired her for one purpose—to care for his family. He didn't have the luxury of thinking about anything else.

He showed her his pastures first. "Most of the year, we rotate our cattle, so they don't overgraze." Although you wouldn't know that from looking at them. The dry fall had hit everyone hard, hay and grain producers included. That led to higher-than-normal prices, which made him think seriously about which bulls he could keep and which ones he'd need to cull.

Droughts always forced ranchers to make hard decisions. At least he was able to supplement their diet with burnt cacti. He'd learned about the plant's high protein content years ago while ranch handing.

Max started to trot back toward him then got distracted by a flock of wild turkeys and took off after them.

"We wean our calves at eight to ten months of age," Monte said. "Then we put them on our pro-performance feed." With how dry it'd been, that cost a pretty penny as well. When he needed to turn a profit more than ever. "About three months later, we start training them—getting them used to being handled, the bucking chute and whatnot."

"Do you keep all your bulls together?"

"Yep."

"They don't fight?"

"Sometimes, least till they establish their pecking order. After that, so long as they've grown up together, they get along well enough."

They passed the tree house he'd built for his girls the summer before. Behind this snaked a creek that swelled in the spring and shrank come August. It cut through the back corner of his land, through the trees, and wound behind the windmill that pumped water from the ground to irrigate his pastures and keep his cattle hydrated. When the well didn't run dry.

"Stables are over there." He pointed to a large red building lined with glassless windows adjacent to the arena. Three of his horses, along with their Shetland and donkey, grazed nearby.

"They're beautiful."

He suppressed a chuckle, amused by the obvious delight in her eyes. "Want to feed them a treat?"

"Absolutely." She must've intended to hide her enthusiasm, because she straightened, and her almost childlike smile turned formal. "Thank you."

With a slight nod, he led the way to the tack room where he kept grooming tools, feed, saddles and other gear. He pulled some keys from his pocket and unbolted the door guarding a large tub of grain, a container filled with peppermints, and an old and partially dehydrated bag of carrots. "Got to keep this area locked up so my girls can't get to it and give the horses a belly ache."

Whinnies and nickers drifted toward them as he deposited a scoopful of grain into a bucket. "My Callie's quicker than lightning. One minute, she's helping me muck the stalls. The next, she's double-fisting candy."

"For herself or the horses?"

"Both."

She followed him to the railing where two of his mares stood, ready and waiting, ears forward, big brown eyes trained on them. "They know what's coming, huh?"

"They hope, isn't that right, Applesauce." He scratched the paint's neck then turned to Evie. "Want to become her new best friend?"

"Sure."

He poured grain into her outstretched hands.

Lady Mule gave a loud hee-haw, startling Evie. "Oh, my. Someone's hungry."

"Always got to get her nose in the action. She's our self-appointed pasture protector. Isn't that right, girl?" He tickled her upper lip.

"Really?"

He nodded. "Donkeys are fighters. Highly territorial, too. They can take on a coyote any day. They also help drive away disease-carrying possums."

"Now that fable about the mule, the monkey and the mountain lion makes much more sense."

"Haven't heard that one."

She relayed the story, initially told to her during the "worst camping experience ever."

"It wouldn't have been so bad if I hadn't attracted every mosquito in Washington State," she said. "Or our parents hadn't made us clean our own fish." She wrinkled her nose. "Suffice to say, sleeping on the ground is not my idea of a relaxing vacation." Her gaze swept across the horizon before landing on his recreational trailer parked near the tree line. "I take it you're a big outdoorsman?"

"The girls' mom and I used to call that old, rusted hunk of metal home. We bought it from an older couple who must not have used it or aired it out in decades. We burned at least a hundred scented candles that first year."

She used to joke that his bulls had better accommodations than they did. He'd told her they were their route to a real home and promised to build her one as soon as their animal athletes began earning more than they ate.

He'd made good on that promise a year later and thought for sure they were steadily heading toward the life they wanted.

Clearly, she'd never shared that dream. Not that he could blame her. Ranch life required a special kind of woman, one with grit, who wasn't worried about breaking a nail or getting mud on her blue jeans.

He cast Evie a sideways glance. Did the woman even own a pair of jeans? Or boots, for that matter?

Chapter Two

When they returned to the house, they were met by Monte's girls, who simultaneously looked identical and vastly different. The one lingering in the open doorway wore a yellow-and-white striped dress with blue flowers, glittery shoes that appeared as sturdy as they were delicate. Her brown hair was secured into two long braids.

The other, and likely the child who double-fisted peppermints, barreled down the stairs like an excited puppy. "I'm Callie." Her wide grin extended to her chestnut eyes, her hair looking like it could use a good brushing and her jeans and T-shirt, gray with a tractor printed in red, in need of a wash. "You our nanny?"

Evie's widened eyes pinged to Monte.

He picked the girl up, swung her in the air, then deposited her, giggling, on her feet. "This is Ms. Bell, and she's here to care for Aunt Martha."

"But not when she's in bed?" The child turned to Evie. By now, her sister had joined her. "Then you'll play with us? And take us to the creek to look for frogs and lizards and go exploring in the forest."

"The forest?"

Monte laughed. "That's what they call that thin stretch of trees bordering our land. Near the camper and gazebo."

"Right." She lowered to the twin's eye level. "I'm sure we'll have plenty of time for adventures." So long as they didn't involve bulls.

As a nontraditional caretaker working for a private company, she found that her job often included tasks related to "daily living." Usually that meant cooking and light housework. While she had nothing against children, she'd heard enough stories from some of her coworkers to leave her apprehensive. Overly concerned family members had nothing on helicopter parents. Thank goodness Monte didn't seem to hold unrealistic expectations—as of yet.

"Luna and I made a fort." Callie flung a hand toward her sister, then leaned closer with a hand cupped around her mouth. "It's private. Girls only. Want me to show you?" She spoke so fast her words blended together.

"Later." Monte's voice was kind but firm. "Let's give Ms. Bell a chance to get settled." He strolled to the rear of Evie's car, as if expecting her to pop her trunk. "I'll grab your things while the girls show you to your room."

"I can get that, but thank you."

Before she could say more, or move his direction, the wild-haired child was tugging her up the porch stairs talking about the "care basket" she and her sister had made. Seemed rude leaving Monte with her luggage—of which, admittedly, she'd brought more than necessary. Yet, dampening the girl's enthusiasm for whatever "surprise" she and her sister had waiting inside didn't feel much better.

Monte's further insistence persuaded her to honor the child's obvious joy. The slight nod of approval he offered as she allowed Callie to pull her up the stairs assured her she'd made the right choice.

Inside was quiet, and the living room cluttered with more toys than when she'd initially met with Monte. A handful of blankets lined the carpet in the hallway.

"This is me and Luna's room." Callie stopped in an opened

doorway to their left and motioned to a space with equal parts dolls, pink frills and plastic animals, tools and trucks. Upon one bed lay a rainbow comforter, the other decorated with horseshoes, stars and spurred boots.

Evie glanced behind her to offer a smile to the other child, clearly much shyer, who lingered nearby. But her breath caught when her gaze landed on Monte, who was standing behind her. He was lugging an overstuffed suitcase in each hand, his biceps straining against his shirt's short sleeves.

"Should've figured my Callie-girl would make a pit stop or two." He rustled Luna's hair, then poked his head into the room. "Ms. Bell and I are scooting on. May want to skedaddle ahead of us, if you're wanting to be there when she sees her welcome gift."

"Oh, yeah!" Chattering with even more animation than before, Callie dashed past them.

Monte grabbed her by the shoulder before she ran off. Holding a finger to his mouth, he glanced toward a slightly cracked door down a ways on the left. "Sh. Aunt Martha may be sleeping."

Callie slumped with a groan as if he'd just told her she couldn't have chocolate for the rest of the month. "But she's always doing that. And she said it's no big deal and that kids will be kids and not to make such a fuss."

Monte frowned.

The child sighed nearly as loudly as she'd groaned. "Yes, sir."

Evie would've laughed—if the entire interchange, and every other moment prior, since she'd arrived on this ranch, wasn't promising a rather exhausting next three weeks. The child had already proven that her legs moved about as quickly as her mouth. On land spanning 250 acres, that could lead to a lot of steps.

If Callie could sneak handfuls of peppermints while working alongside her dad in the stables, how long would it take her to wander out among the bulls while Evie tended to her great-aunt?

If this assignment proved more challenging than Evie could manage, would she lose her job?

They rounded the corner to find Callie hopping onto and off the bottom step of wooden, retractable railless stairs that led, she presumed, to the attic. She glanced around, then to Monte, who'd stopped beside his daughter, then to the rectangular opening above her.

"Out of the way, munchkin." Monte set one of the suitcases down and moved the child aside.

Evie shivered as thoughts of cobwebs and spiders lurking in corners and creeping across the floor came to mind. *Please tell me that's not where I'll be staying.*

Her concern must've shown on her face, because Monte said, "Don't worry. You won't be holed up in some dark corner. I turned the attic into a comfortable guest room, with carpet, brightly painted walls, a nice reading nook and plenty of window space. Even installed a half bath."

She raised her eyebrows. "Really?"

He nodded. "Hope you won't mind using the one down here for showers."

"Not at all." She watched as he began lugging her belongings up the stairs, understanding why he'd insisted on carrying everything for her. And she was quite grateful.

She wasn't sure how many more "surprises" she could handle. Sent to a town that was probably occupied by fewer people than her old high school and hours from the nearest shopping mall, or movie theater for that matter. To stay on a ranch. That raised bulls that bucked. To help care for two adorable little girls, one of whom would exhaust a day care's entire, highly caffeinated staff.

And sleep in what Mr. Cowboy assured her was an upscaled attic, but an attic just the same.

She followed after him and the girls.

Pausing to preemptively hide whatever grimace might try to force through a professionally appropriate smile, she sucked in a breath and poked her head through the opening.

Her tense shoulders relaxed with her exhale. A genuine smile took form as she surveyed the cozy and aesthetically pleasing space. "Lovely."

Lace-trimmed curtains matched the painted walls, three of which were pink, the fourth, a rich burgundy. A bench seat topped with a long, floral cushion stretched beneath the far window, and various books filled corner shelves. A pink and lavender quilt with blue trim was spread across a queen-size bed. Decorative pillows added to its charm, and rather than the musty smell she'd feared, the room carried a slight scent of lemon and cedar.

Monte grinned and offered a hand. She took it, his skin, warm and rough against hers, sending a jolt of electricity through her. Heat rushed to her face as she tried to break contact as soon as possible.

"Are you hot?"

Evie turned to find Callie standing beside her, studying her. "What?"

"Your face is red, like mine gets when I run real fast for a long time."

That caused her cheeks to flush even more. Thankfully, Monte either thought nothing of the question or had missed it entirely, because he began talking about how he turned the space into a livable loft.

"I added those dormer windows to bump up the ceiling height and brighten the room." He pointed. "A contractor buddy helped me get the flooring up to code."

"Impressive."

She feigned interest as he continued talking about bridging joists, rerouting ventilation, and other renovation details she didn't understand. Then he shifted to why she came.

"I made a binder of about everything you need to know in regard to my aunt, the girls and the ranch." He grabbed it off her bedside table and handed it over. "We'd be much obliged if you'd help us with cooking and basic household chores. It's more than Aunt Martha can manage of late."

"Understandable."

"I could really use a hand getting the girls ready and off to preschool in the mornings. Aunt Martha will need you to drive her to her treatments in Houston once a week. Those are near all-day deals. Her platelet count was pretty low last time. Not sure she'll be up for her next dose of chemo."

"Okay."

"Doc'll be out Wednesday or Thursday to draw blood."

"Wow. That's quite a drive. I'm impressed."

"He's local—her regular physician. The treatment center's pretty good about letting her do whatever she can, here in Sage Creek."

"That's great." Evie flipped through the binder as he thoroughly explained his aunt's care plan and the family's typical routine.

"May want to snag some time before supper to rest from your drive."

"I appreciate that."

He turned to his daughters. "While you two clean the tornado you made below."

"What about the surprise?" Callie asked, Luna all bright-eyed by her side.

"Totally forgot." One hand resting on his belt buckle, he glanced about. "Where'd you two put it?"

Callie cupped a hand around her mouth and whispered, "Somewhere secret." She looked at Evie. "Close your eyes."

She complied, her smile expanding at the sound of little feet scurrying across the carpet. After this, she heard whispered bickering, a firm, "Girls," from Monte, and Callie's instructions to open her eyes on the count of three.

She did, laughing at their, "Surprise." The most delightful giggles followed as the twins gave over a basket filled with snowflakes cut from paper, hand-drawn pictures, slices of gum, a partially burned candle and a few other random items. They must have scoured the house in search of "treasures" to give her.

How precious.

"Do you like it?" Callie bounced on the balls of her feet.

"I absolutely love it." Her gaze shot to Monte, and her breath caught to find him watching her with an intensity that turned her insides to jelly.

That was yet another reason she was grateful she'd soon be away from this ranch—and this much too handsome cowboy.

The longer she stayed, the less likely she'd leave with her heart intact.

The oven timer dinged. Monte exchanged the steaming casserole with a sheet of prebaked biscuits. His mouth watered as he inhaled the cheesy-garlicky steam rising from the dish.

He glanced into the living room to find Luna picking up scattered pieces to a board game while her sister stacked a series of rectangular blocks end on end.

Standing in the archway, he crossed his arms. "Callie, that doesn't look like cleaning up to me."

She glanced up. "Oh. I forgot." Her wide-eyed look of surprise indicated she was telling the truth.

That girl could get distracted walking from the couch to the television.

He surveyed the remaining mess. Experience told him Luna had already tackled more than her fair share. With that assumption, he excused her to let Evie and Aunt Martha know supper was almost ready.

He turned to Callie. "Do what you can now. You can finish the rest after we eat."

"By myself?"

"Yep. That way you can catch up with what your sister already did."

Slumping with a sigh and frown, she began tossing her blocks into their tub, making her frustration known with every overdramatic clunk.

Suppressing a chuckle that otherwise would only irritate his daughter further, he shook his head and went to the pantry for a couple cans of green beans and emptied them into a bowl. He was removing them from the microwave when the twins entered with their aunt.

He greeted Aunt Martha with a kiss on the cheek. "How was your nap?"

"Much longer than I expected." Yet, she still looked tired, or discouraged.

Probably both. Considering the dark place he'd started to slip into upon hearing her cancer had returned, he could understand. But the more positive they stayed, the greater their strength and perseverance for the long battle ahead.

"The more rest the better, right?" He beat her to the table and pulled out her chair.

She quirked an eyebrow, humor dancing in her eyes. "What's good for the goose? Because it seems to me you've been burning the candle at both ends and in the middle besides."

He laughed. "Nah. A man can hardly call it work when he's doing what he loves." The last thing he wanted was for her to start worrying about him.

He noted her frown as she watched him place food on the table. Fearing she might feel guilty that she hadn't been the

one to prepare it, he told her about Evie's arrival. This initiated an animated retelling of the twins' surprise from Callie.

"Sorry to keep you waiting."

He turned as Evie entered, captivated by her almost shy
smile. She'd pulled her hair up in a messy bun, a few streaked,
strawberry blond strands framing her face. Although she wore
the same blouse and slacks she'd arrived in, without the blazer,
her trim yet curvy form was more noticeable. And her ap-
parent embarrassment at thinking she'd arrived late added a
beautiful flush to her cheeks.

The same delicate blush he'd caught in the loft. One he
wasn't any more comfortable with, nor how it affected him,
now than he had been then.

He cleared his throat and raked a hand through his hatless
hair. "Perfect timing." He introduced her to his aunt.

"Pleasure to meet you." Evie's smile widened as she approached his aunt initiating a handshake.

"Thank you for coming all this way," his aunt said. "How
was your drive?"

"Easy-peasy. No road work or traffic between here and
Dallas."

Monte raised his eyebrows. "Now, that's a surprise. Seems
every time I'm on I-35, the DOT's doing something."

Callie frowned. "A dot?"

He laughed. "Department of Transportation."

"Oh." This led to a plethora of questions that shifted to one
of Callie's obsessions—tractors and other heavy machinery.
Somehow this morphed into a rather extensive listing of various nicknames she'd heard.

"Daddy calls me his little Cowpoke." She grinned. "Cuz
I'm so tough, right, Daddy?"

"Stiffer than leather." He ruffled her hair.

"And Luna likes to smell books."

"Do not." Her sister crossed her arms with a pout.

"Do so." Callie swiped her hair away from her face with her forearm. "Just ask Ms. Lucy."

He narrowed his gaze on the child. "What Ms. Lucy says is that your sister is a bookworm. And you know good and well she speaks the words in love."

Callie huffed. "Reading is stupid and boring. That's why I don't want to go to school. Cuz they have to do boring stuff and sit behind a desk all day. You don't even get snacks when you want. Plus, Max will miss me."

Aunt Martha chuckled. "I'm sure he'll survive."

The child frowned. "Who will he play with?"

"He'll have Finn, dear." The woman's hand trembled slightly as she lifted her glass.

Callie shook her head. "He'll be too busy minding the bulls with Daddy. And you'll just stay in bed."

Aunt Martha flinched, and her gaze dropped to her largely untouched plate.

"Callie Rose Bowman." Monte's tone was firm.

"But it's true." Tears filled the girl's eyes, suggesting she'd merely intended to state facts as she saw them, not to be rude.

She still needed to learn to use a filter. His aunt felt bad enough about her inability to do more for the girls.

"I said enough." He looked around. "Shall we bless the food?" When everyone had bowed their heads, he led them in prayer, which, based on the thump-thump-thumping coming from Callie's direction, must've exceeded her patience level.

As usual.

"This kitchen is lovely." Evie's gaze swept the room, lingering on the hand-embroidered towel hanging from the stove handle. It was green with lace trim, and a reindeer stitched in silver thread.

"Mostly thanks to Aunt Martha's loving touch." Although, Erin, his ex-wife, had chosen the paint colors—white cabinets and cupboards set against celery green walls, his aunt had sewn the checkered and lace curtains.

On the wooden countertop left of the sink, a wicker basket she'd found at a garage sale held fruit. Next to this, a ceramic crock she'd painted during a ladies' church event held various cooking utensils. She'd purchased the tall glass canisters that were now filled with various foodstuff at the local pawn shop.

Aunt Martha took a sip of her drink. "Where are you from, Evie?"

"Holland, Michigan."

"Your folks still there?" He spooned green beans on his girls' plates with a look that communicated that he expected them to eat them.

She nodded. "Although at this precise moment, they're with my siblings—I've got three—hiking the Myakka Trail in Florida."

Aunt Martha looked up, lowering the fork that never quite made it to her mouth. "I imagine winters are quite lovely there. I'm sorry you couldn't join them."

Did she worry she'd cost the woman her vacation? Thankfully, Evie refuted that idea quickly enough.

"I could have." She spread butter onto her biscuit. "If I'd wanted to trade nice crisp sheets for a musty old sleeping bag."

Callie studied her with a tilt of her head. "What does that mean?"

Evie shifted in her seat and gave a nervous laugh. "Guess I'm just not the roughing-it type."

"I believe what she's saying is that she'd prefer to spend her nights in some posh hotel somewhere with Wi-Fi and air-conditioning," Monte said. Rather than on the land the good Lord gave them. "That the gist of it?"

She grinned. "Exactly."

"Yet here you are. On a ranch." He'd intended his tone to hold more of a teasing lilt. Her look of surprise indicated he'd failed. Yet, neither of them could deny this wasn't their first choice. He'd asked New Day Caregivers to send someone more accustomed to country living. And he suspected, Evie preferred much more concrete and the lifestyle that tended to accompany it.

They'd both have to make the best of a less than ideal situation for the next few weeks. He'd be happy so long as she cared for Aunt Martha and the girls. It didn't take an animal science degree to do that. Just a compassionate heart, an attentive eye and basic medical knowledge, all of which her field already required.

"Maybe God wants us to teach her how to have fun." Callie gave one quick nod. "Cuz hotels are even boringer than school."

He fought to contain his grin. "Is that a fact?"

"Uh-huh. Cuz you have to be quiet and not jump or run in the halls or up and down the stairs, unless all the old people are still awake."

Evie laughed. "You have a point." Her gaze shot to Monte, catching him watching her.

He quickly focused on his plate. "How long you been working as a traveling caregiver?"

"Almost three years now."

Aunt Martha moved her green beans around her plate. "I bet you've visited some interesting places."

"It's been a fun way to explore the United States."

"I can do twenty pushups," Callie said. "Want to see?" She sprang to her feet and threw herself on the floor before Evie could respond.

"That's enough." Monte softened his firm voice with kindness.

"Yes, sir." Her words came out on a loud exhale as she marched back to the table.

When she launched into a story about how she was the fastest kid in her Sunday school class, Monte nudged her plate toward her. "Eat your supper, now. And hold your words." While he didn't mind her enthusiasm one bit—rather enjoyed it, actually—he knew the child could wear other people's ears out.

"Our little Callie likes to talk." Aunt Martha unfolded her napkin and spread it across her lap. "Isn't that right, sweet pea."

She nodded, seeming not the least bothered by the reprimand. "Cuz I've got so much stuff bouncing around in my head." She patted her skull. "That can be hard to keep in sometimes. But Ms. Lucy said that's when I can use my strength. Said if I can barrel race and mutton bust with the best of them—I'm not the best yet, but Daddy says I will be, soon 'nuff. And Ms. Lucy says if I can rodeo as good as I do, then I can keep my thoughts in my head no matter how hard they're fighting to come out."

Evie laughed. "I see." She swallowed a mouthful of food. "What's a mutton bust?"

Luna's head snapped up.

Callie's brow furrowed. "You don't know for real, Ms. Evie? Or are you joshing us?"

"Can't say that I do."

A few hours ago, that might've surprised Monte. But after her questions regarding bulls and rough stock, he probably would've been stunned if she had known.

The child opened her mouth to say more, but Monte raised a hand, palm out. "How about you give your sister a chance to speak, darling."

Callie slumped with a huff, and soon her feet took to swinging again.

That child was sure to keep Evie on her toes—an unsettling thought considering her lack of experience with children and ranches. Hopefully, common sense would override any ignorance that could otherwise prove dangerous.

Monte offered his other daughter a warm smile. "Luna, want to answer Ms. Evie's question?"

"Yes, sir." She spoke a decibel above a whisper. "Mutton busting is where you try to stay on a sheep—"

"Bareback." Callie grinned.

Evie's eyebrows shot up. "That must be quite challenging."

Luna shrugged. "You only have to stay on for six seconds."

"'Cept Luna and I haven't done that. But I'm close, right, Daddy?"

"You both are." He wiped his mouth with his napkin. "Keep strengthening your grip swinging from tree branches, caterpillar." He scooped up a forkful of casserole, a string of cheese trailing from his plate.

"You should come watch us," Callie said.

Monte swallowed a bite of food. "Doubt she'll be here long enough for that."

"Does that make you sad?"

"What?" She looked from the child to Monte, to his aunt, then back to Monte. "Oh, yes, of course. That was so kind of you to invite me." She tore off a chunk of biscuit. "I've never been to a rodeo."

Monte's jaw went slack.

Then Callie gave a soft giggle that warmed his heart. "You're being silly. Ain't you?"

"Aren't," Monte corrected, although he was equally interested in the answer.

Callie sighed. "Are-en-t you?"

Evie shifted and occupied herself with her food. "Nope. I'm serious."

"Not even to see the bull riding or barrel racing or steer roping or nothing?"

She shook her head.

The girl stared at her as if she'd said she'd spent the prior years of her life locked up within her house or something.

Monte would've laughed if not so flabbergasted himself. But he wasn't entirely surprised, considering all her questions while touring the property.

"Well, now." Aunt Martha quirked an eye at him. "Seems we've got to do something about that. Don't you agree?"

"Yes! Yes! Yes!" Callie bounced in her seat, and Luna brightened.

Monte's pulse kicked up a notch. He had a strong feeling he wouldn't like where his aunt was steering the conversation.

He knew she worried about his rather pathetic social life and longed to see him married—for his sake and the girls'. Was that why she wanted him to take Evie to the rodeo—to force them to spend more time together? Then again, she had to realize her caregiver wouldn't stick around long.

He was probably overthinking Aunt Martha's suggestion.

"Could be a good opportunity to take some of your new classics to the Christmas rodeo." Aunt Martha looked at Evie. "That's what they call four-year-old bulls." She resumed eye contact with Monte. "Get them used to a new arena and a crowd."

"Not sure a charity event's the best place to debut them."

His aunt gave a one-shoulder shrug. "May not meet any potential sponsors, but the girls would sure have a great time."

"I'm not comfortable leaving you home alone that long."

"I'll be fine." She flicked a hand. "Like Callie said, I'll probably do a lot of sleeping anyway. And there's always a ranch hand close by, if I need anything."

"Even so."

"I'll reach out to Lucy. She's been bugging me about watching old musicals with her, anyway. This would be a great way for you to build memories with the girls while giving Evie a taste of cowboy culture, holiday-style."

He scratched his jaw, looking from his girls, to Evie, to his aunt, to his girls, then back to his aunt. Aunt Martha was right about the twins. He'd been much too busy and distracted, of late. Regardless of the reason, his girls needed their dad.

He was all for a fun weekend with them both. He wasn't so sure how he felt about Evie tagging along. But his aunt would never let her stay, not when Evie was the reason for the idea.

Luna clasped folded hands beneath her chin. "Can we, Daddy? Please?"

Why was it so hard to tell that child no when she turned those big chestnut eyes his direction? Maybe because she rarely asked for much. Unlike her sister, who had about ten requests for every situation.

He sighed. "I'll see what I can do."

"And Ms. Evie, too?" Callie asked.

He looked at her, trying unsuccessfully to gauge her feelings on the matter. "If she'd like."

Callie sprang from her chair and hurried to Evie's side. "Do you? It's real fun. They've got clowns and horses and cookie decorating with lots of different colored frosting and sprinkles and stuff. And Daddy always buys us corn dogs for supper."

Aunt Martha caught her eye. "Seems a good opportunity for you and the girls to bond."

Way to guilt the woman into accepting. He'd been too frustrated with himself to realize he'd wanted to know her interest level.

"Sure." She forked a cheese-covered noodle. "That sounds like fun."

"Yay!" Callie jumped up and down, fist pumping the air.

Monte urged the child back to her seat. "I'll make lodging arrangements."

Why did the thought of spending a full weekend with Evie leave him feeling so off-kilter? So what that she was the most beautiful woman he'd encountered in some time, even more so than his ex, if he were being honest. And just as averse to his way of life.

Chapter Three

The next morning, Evie descended the stairs to find cartoons playing on the television in the living room and Monte and the girls in the kitchen. The smell of fresh brewed coffee and hot chocolate made Evie crave a mocha. Maybe she could take the twins to that cute café/bookstore she'd seen on Main Street.

Would Monte want to join them? The thought sent an unwelcome flutter through her midsection, which she quickly shut down. She didn't need to start feeding her attraction to the man by entertaining absurd questions. Besides, she was here to help with the aunt and children so he could focus on his ranch.

She paused in the archway separating the living room and kitchen to watch him and the girls. The children's behavior and bedclothes differentiated them. Callie, dressed in a navy and superhero-print nightgown, spoke fast and hopped from one foot to the next. Luna sat quietly at the table coloring a snowman picture. She wore gradient pink and purple pj's decorated with sparkly stars.

Monte looked all cowboy in his jeans, boots and flannel shirt. He was humming "Jingle Bell Rock." His playfulness only added to his appeal.

He opened the fridge and moved some items around, Callie lingering at his side.

"Sorry, nugget." Facing her, he tapped her on the nose.

"Guess y'all ate the last of the French toast sticks. I can nuke some of the breakfast burritos the church gals brought over."

Callie groaned. "Those are yucky."

"You liked them well enough Sunday."

"I changed my mind."

"Cereal it is."

"But we don't have any good kinds." Her tone carried a whine.

"Then you must not be that hungry."

"Yogurt?"

He opened the fridge again, grabbed a tub, popped the lid and sniffed. "Whew. That's rancid." He tossed it in the nearby trash can. "Guess we're out of that, too."

"Aw!" She fisted her hands at her sides. "We never have anything to eat."

Evie bit the inside of her lip to keep from laughing. Apparently, the child hadn't seen all the filled food containers in the fridge.

Monte's phone rang. He pulled it from his back pocket and glanced at the screen.

She stepped into the room. "I can make French toast sticks."

He turned toward her with what looked like a smile tinged with gratitude. "Thank you. And good morning." His cell chirped again. "I need to take this." He tapped his screen on his way to the pantry. "Hey, Jesse. Thanks for returning my call."

He retrieved a loaf of bread and set it on the counter. "Nope. No fires to put out. Just wanted to let you know I won't be around this weekend. I'll keep my cell handy, should you need anything."

He placed a large bowl from the cupboard onto the counter, stuck a wooden spoon inside it, and motioned Evie over.

With a nod, she set out the remaining ingredients.

"Oh, I'm sure they will." Phone to his ear, he pulled a pocket notebook from the junk drawer and started flipping through the pages. "They've never been to one of these holiday shin-digs. Guess that tells you how long it's been for me, huh? Fig-ured, as long as we're going, may as well bring some of my bulls."

He started talking about bucking chute etiquette, bull inten-sity and other things Evie assumed were related to the rodeo.

Like the one he'd asked her to attend.

Only he hadn't. His aunt had forced the invite, and of course Monte had given in. He probably didn't want to be rude.

She doubted he was thrilled to have her tagging along. Why did that fact leave her with a hint of disappointment? It wasn't like she wanted to go, either.

Except she did. But only for the new experience, not be-cause her pulse spiked whenever the cowboy's brown eyes held hers. Or she watched them soften when he spoke to his daugh-ters, or twinkle with mirth when they said something funny.

What had gotten into her? She was here to fulfill a role, for a short period at that, not to fall for a man she'd never see again once she left Sage Creek.

"Want me to get you a frying pan?"

She startled at Monte's voice, then blushed when she real-ized she'd been standing there lost in preposterous thoughts.

Releasing the spoon, she cleared her throat and placed slices of bread onto a cutting board beside the sink. "I got a little distracted." *Thinking about you, as absurd as that is.*

Although he *was* handsome. There was nothing wrong with acknowledging that.

So long as she remained wise and professional—more non-chalant than elevated heart rate.

He refilled his coffee cup and leaned back against the coun-ter, legs crossed at the ankles. "The girls have a Christmas party this afternoon. At their new preschool. The director in-vited them. Said it could help them feel more comfortable for their first day."

"How thoughtful."

He nodded. "Aunt Martha and the ladies from church will want pictures. Think you can get them dolled up a bit?"

"Sure."

"Luna will comply with no problem. She loves anything frilly. Callie might take some cajoling. Feel free to bribe her with a visit to the 'forest' after. Once she's changed, of course, which she'll probably do the minute we get back."

"Behind the gazebo?"

"Yep. Just keep them away from the water."

"Okay. Anywhere else off-limits?"

"Nope. Other than the creek, so long as you're with them, they can pretty much go wherever you're comfortable. Don't figure you'll be venturing near the bulls?" His tone held a teasing lilt.

She laughed. "Absolutely not."

"Expect Callie to tiptoe right up to whatever boundary line you set. But she'll mind you so long as you're firm and consistent. You'll never have to worry about Luna. She came into the world looking for rules to follow."

He watched as Callie lined stones across the wood floor. "I doubt their party will last more than a couple hours. Supper's at six. Know how to fry chicken?"

"Probably not as well as Aunt Martha, but yeah."

"If you can cook even half as well as her, we'll eat good tonight." Taking a sip of his coffee, he regarded her with mirthfilled eyes.

This lighthearted side of him, wrapped up in his rugged cowboy exterior, left her even more unsettled than his steady gaze.

He glanced at Luna, his expression tender as he watched her color. "The girls may want to hang with me while I do chores this afternoon."

"You're okay with that?"

"May help if you stayed with them, but yeah. They can help me muck a stall and feed the animals. They'll probably want a turn on the ATV when I drag the arena. I've got some cowboys coming to ride some of my mature bulls. Practice for everyone involved. If that interests you, you're welcome to watch."

Her eyes widened as thoughts of men getting stomped on flashed through her mind. "That sounds dangerous."

"So's driving through rush hour traffic in Dallas, yet you survived." Laughter lines crinkled around his eyes. "But don't worry. I won't force you to ride. Least, not this early in your stay."

Her heart gave an unexpected lurch at his playful banter, which seemed to have replaced the edge he'd displayed when she first arrived. Hopefully that meant that he was beginning to feel more comfortable with her as a caregiver. Walking beside a family member fighting cancer was hard enough. She fully intended to lessen that load however she could.

Her demonstrating her competency would reduce his concerns.

Regardless, the handsome cowboy had alerted her to something. If she continued working with New Day, she'd need to stick with elderly patients in the future. And work extra hard at maintaining her professional demeanor in the present.

Because seeing the blend of warmth and strength with which Monte interacted with his girls was threatening to turn her insides into mush.

Good-looking, she could handle. Attractive merged with playful affection was another matter.

She finished making breakfast, the scent of cinnamon and butter filling the air, while the girls played a modified game of checkers.

After a few more phone calls, Monte snagged a couple French toast sticks, and drizzled them with enough syrup to create soup. Taking a bite, he raised his eyebrows. "Not bad."

"Yeah?"

He nodded. "Might even be a match for Aunt Martha's." He glanced through the archway, his lips twitching toward a smile. "Don't tell her I said that."

Her grin emerged before she could cover her enthusiasm with a nonchalant smile. "Your secret is safe with me."

He popped the last of his rushed breakfast into his mouth and washed it down with a swig of coffee. Depositing his dishes in the sink, he glanced at the time on the microwave. "Guess I best get going."

Callie slid from her chair and rushed over. "Me, too, Daddy?"

He scooped her up. "Not this time, Cowpoke." With her feet dangling, he kissed her neck, causing the child to giggle and squirm. "I'm running behind this morning." He deposited her back on her feet.

"But I can help."

"Oh, I'm sure you'd be a help, all right." He shot Evie a wink, sending a jolt through her. "But I think it's best if you, Luna and Ms. Bell get more acquainted."

She frowned. "We already did. Last night at supper."

Evie didn't take the child's statement personally. Of course, she'd want to spend time with her father. She adored him and he her. But the better she and the girls got along, the easier her job would be—and the more confidence Monte would hold in her abilities.

"We'll be together plenty today." He wrapped an arm around her waist, gave a squeeze, then kissed her and Luna goodbye.

Once the twins finished eating, Evie sent them to the bathroom to wash the syrup from their hands and faces, and for Callie, out of her hair. Then she walked down the hall to check on Martha.

The door stood ajar, and the woman sat propped up in bed reading.

Evie knocked softly. "Good morning, ma'am. Can I get

you anything? Juice or a banana?" Both should be easy on her stomach, if she felt queasy.

"Not at the moment, but thank you." She looked tired. Frail.

Respecting her space, Evie nodded and slipped away. She caught a glimpse of Callie as she walked past the bathroom. The child stood gripping the sink, face under the faucet, water dripping off her loose strands of hair.

Evie frowned. "No more, please."

Callie looked at her as droplets continued plunk-plunk-plunking on the floor. "But I'm thirsty."

"Then come finish your juice. After you clean up the puddle growing beneath you."

This wasn't a great sign regarding how the rest of her day might proceed.

Callie sighed and turned off the water. "Okay. But then will you play with me?"

Evie smiled. "Sure. What would you like to play?"

"Pick-up sticks. No, stack the boxes. Wait! Go Fish!"

"My brothers and sisters and I used to play that a lot when we were growing up."

"Really?

She nodded, and once Callie had cleaned her mess, followed the child to the cupboards beneath the television. Inside, puzzles and board games were stacked on top of tubs of toys. An endearing image came to mind of Monte and his girls gathered around a board game.

She could tell those girls, and his aunt, were his entire world. He'd probably been an attentive and loyal husband as well. What had happened with his ex-wife? And why had he remained single?

More importantly, why did her brain wonder about things that weren't any of her business?

"Here it is!" Holding the cards high, Callie skipped into the kitchen and climbed onto a chair. Luna followed and sat beside Evie, periodically casting her the most adorable, shy smile.

The twins were as different as sisters could be. That was a good thing. Two Callies could about wear a person into the ground. Although Evie had to admit, she found the child delightful. So full of life and joy. Traits Luna balanced with her quiet, observant nature.

Curiosity sparked in Luna's eyes. "You have brothers and sisters?"

Warmth spread through Evie's chest. That was the first time the sweet child had initiated conversation with her since she arrived. Was she feeling more comfortable?

Evie shuffled the cards with a nod. "Two older brothers and a younger sister."

"Do you still play with them?" Seemed fitting Callie would ask that.

"In a way, I suppose."

"And your daddy?"

"Over the holidays. Trivia, mostly. Only I'm not very good."

Callie studied her. "Does that mean you lose?"

She laughed. "Pretty much. My brother, on the other hand, is like a walking library."

Luna's eyes lit up. "I love the library. Some days, Aunt Martha takes us to story time."

"Only not anymore." Callie frowned and crossed her arms. "Cuz she's always so tired and stuff."

Evie placed a hand on her shoulder. "That's hard."

She nodded. "But she's going to get better now that you're here. Daddy says that's why you came."

Wow. No pressure there.

She always felt uncomfortable with these types of conversations, especially with children. They were almost as difficult as those that occurred when patients were placed on hospice. She hoped that wouldn't occur here. In the meantime, Evie needed God's guidance on how to support this family amid all the uncertainty they faced.

That always felt like a heavy assignment.

Her training had taught her that the best way she could comfort a person was to remain present. That she could do.

And she could pray.

She had just finished asking God to encase each of the Bowmans in His love when Callie shifted to talking about the upcoming rodeo.

She jutted her chin. "I'm going to hold on to my sheep for all six seconds. I've been making my grip strong. That's what they call it when you can hold on to stuff for a long time." She opened and closed her hand. "Want me to show you?" She grasped onto Evie's arm and squeezed so tightly her face scrunched up.

Evie fought to hide her amusement. "Impressive."

Callie grinned and refocused on their game.

After a few rounds of Go Fish, the girls decided to play school with their stuffed animals. This lasted about fifteen minutes before they asked to watch their "absolutest-favorite cartoon ever!" Assured their father wouldn't mind and anxious to tackle some housework, since that was part of her job, Evie agreed.

She cleaned the kitchen and dusted the living room before the girls decided to make a fort from furniture, couch cushions and sheets.

Callie peered up at her with eyes filled with such innocence, the look had to be well-rehearsed. Especially considering the context. "Daddy lets us so long as we put everything back when we're done."

That was probably the best activity to keep the little ball of energy occupied for any length of time—both in the construction and cleanup.

This also could provide the bribe Monte suggested Callie might need to don the outfit he wanted her to wear for the Christmas party. "After you put on the clothes your dad laid out on your beds and brush your teeth and hair."

Luna scampered off, with a disgruntled Callie lagging behind.

Those girls were as energetic as they were adorable. How had Monte managed them by himself after Tracy left?

No wonder he'd expressed such urgency that New Day Caregivers find a temporary fill-in.

With the children well entertained in their fort, filled with books, iPad, plastic and stuffed animals, and numerous pillows, Evie entered the kitchen to check the fridge and pantry for supper ingredients.

She'd clean up their disaster and tackle the mound of laundry overflowing the hamper while they were at the party. Finding the meat drawer bare, she pulled chicken legs from the freezer and set them in a sink of water to thaw.

After surveying his supply of veggies and salad fixings, she shot Monte a text offering a few options for sides.

Her phone dinged a response: Any of those sound great. The girls will probably ask for pickles. You'll find some of Aunt Martha's home-canned in the pantry.

Sounds delicious.

A loud crash came from somewhere outside the kitchen. Dropping her cell on the counter, she hurried into the living room. "Luna? Callie?" She lifted a corner of their fort and peered inside to find them lying on their bellies, Luna focused on a book while her sister watched something on her iPad.

Evie's chest tightened. Martha.

She raced down the hall and knocked on the woman's partially opened door. "Ma'am?" She stepped inside and surveyed the empty and disheveled bed. Where had she—the bathroom.

"Ma'am, are you all right?"

She was sitting on the floor, face in her hands. Beside her was an overturned countertop organizer, its contents spilled out. Intermixed with this lay shattered pieces of a small, ceramic cactus.

Evie rushed to her side and placed an arm around her shoulders. "What happened?"

Martha straightened with a visible breath. Surveying the mess all around her, she shook her head. "I got dizzy and reached out to steady myself and…and… I'm so sorry." She struggled to stand. "I'll clean this up."

Supporting her beneath her elbows, Evie helped her to her feet. "No big deal. I'll take care of it." She kept her voice soft, soothing. "Let's get you back to bed."

Martha hesitated, like she wanted to protest. Poor woman had probably spent so much time tending for others, she didn't quite know how to respond on the receiving end. But with her feeling even slightly lightheaded, Evie wasn't comfortable with her up and moving around.

She guided her back to her room.

"I think I'd rather sit in my chair, if you don't mind."

"Of course." Evie walked with her to the dusty rose recliner tucked in the corner beside the window and helped her get settled. "You cold?"

"A bit."

Evie grabbed a knitted throw blanket from a wicker basket nearby and laid it across Martha's lap. "How about I make you some chicken broth?"

"Maybe you should."

The woman wasn't up to eating but likely understood, especially after her fall, her need for calories. Not that there were many in broth, but that was better than nothing.

Evie dashed back into the kitchen. Glancing at the girls' fort en route, she paused to listen to Callie's cartoon, emanating from beneath it. And most likely, Luna still lay stretched out beside her, flipping the pages of one of the many books she'd brought in.

Five minutes later, Evie carried a steaming bowl and half a sleeve of saltines to Martha. Sensing her sorrow, she sat on the edge of her bed and waited, should Martha want to speak.

She'd found, if one waited long enough, without pushing or prodding, others often opened up. This proved true in this instance as well, because just when she was about to excuse herself, Martha began to speak.

"I'm not normally this weepy." She offered a hint of a smile.

"Considering the circumstances, I'd say it's normal—and healthy—to shed a few tears now and again."

Martha studied her for a moment then gave a slight nod. "I suppose you're right. And here, in my room, Lord knows I've done that."

Evie caught the words left unspoken: But not in front of Monte and the children. That was relatively common, as well. Those with cancer often hid their own pain so as to not cause their family further distress, while their loved ones did the same. Unfortunately, that tended to leave everyone alone in their struggle.

But that was why Evie was here. While it wasn't her place to advise them on how to handle the situation or their relationships, she could listen, without judgement or offering unsolicited advice. And so, asking God to pour His love through her, she listened as Martha shared some of her fears and anxieties.

Evie glanced at the clock on the bedside table. She was as reluctant to end what felt like a sacred conversation as she was to leave the twins unattended for long.

Thankfully, the woman made the decision for her. She held up a nearby book on deepening one's intimacy with Christ. "If you don't mind, I think I'll catch up on some reading."

"Not at all." Evie smiled, gave the woman's shoulder a gentle squeeze, and strolled out of the room.

She stopped at the end of the hallway and cocked an ear. Silence.

With what she knew of Callie, that couldn't be a good sign.

"Girls?" She entered the living room and peered beneath their fort. Lots of toys and books. No children.

She hurried down the hall. They weren't in their bedroom, either.

"Is everything all right?" Martha asked from her opened doorway.

Evie forced a confident smile. "Yes, ma'am. I need to take care of something real quick." *Like making sure the girls hadn't wandered into one of the pastures with the bulls or somewhere else equally dangerous.*

Evie dashed out of the house and down the porch steps, grateful Monte wasn't in sight. She'd hate for him to see her without the kids and ask about them. Telling him she had no idea certainly wouldn't earn her points in the trust department.

And if the twins had wandered into one of the pastures with the bulls...

She didn't want to think about that.

Unfortunately, with the way her experience here had been going, Martha would probably once again get dizzy and fall—while Evie was searching for Monte's missing children.

Scanning the visible property, Evie cupped her hands around her mouth and called out to the twins.

First real day on the job, and she'd already lost them. Surely Monte knew how challenging Callie was! He'd been parenting her for five years, after all. Unless he always had others, like the ladies from church, a nanny, or someone from a caregiving service to rely on. Even so, the child had to have slipped away from the most attentive adults a time or two—or twenty.

Evie paused and held her breath. She heard their voices.

Following the high-pitched sound—laughter merged with hollering—she raced around the house then froze.

Callie stood over a mud-filled plastic pool, looking as if she'd been swimming in the stuff. And Luna, who was running toward Evie, crying, had smears on her face, droplets on her dress, and globs in her hair. The shivering child looked like she'd lost a mud fight.

Based on Callie's hands, coated to past her wrists, that was precisely what had occurred.

And with less than twenty minutes before their father would arrive to take them to their party. To make matters worse—as if that were possible—Max was covered in mud as well and chose that very moment to try to shake it off.

Catching Evie in the spray.

She should've known better than to wear her white pants.

Taking in a deep, slow breath, she counted to four, then exhaled. She dropped to one knee in front of Luna, who now stood before her, and placed a hand on her shoulder. "What happened, sweetie?" Not that figuring that out took any kind of sleuthing.

Thank goodness today was relatively warm, one of the blessings of the south.

The little one leaned into her, causing moisture, likely a lovely shade of brown, to seep into her pink shirt as drips from the child's hair snaked their way to Evie's elbow. "Callie got me dirty."

Evie straightened, at a complete loss for words.

Callie seemed momentarily tongue-tied as well, although she came up with a story soon enough. "We were pretending to be pigs, and—"

"No, I wasn't." Luna stomped a foot.

"Yuh-huh!"

"Enough." Evie spoke with more force than she'd intended, and both girls stared at her with wide eyes. "Let's get you both washed up." Maybe if she worked quickly, and Monte was delayed, she could get the girls scrubbed clean and changed before their father arrived.

Without tracking mud through the house. Had this been summer, she would've simply hosed the girls off.

The sound of someone behind her clearing their throat a moment later indicated it was too late for that.

Evie turned around to find Monte glaring at her. "I can explain."

He looked from her to Luna, whose teeth were chattering, to Callie, both girls covered in mud, then back to Evie. "I'd love to hear you try."

He crossed his arms, and a muscle in his jaw twitched.

Evie's mind went blank.

"Daddy." With an all-out sob that was likely part princess, Luna raced into his arms.

He swept her up and held her close as she quickly relayed her version of the situation, barely pausing to suck in a stuttered breath. Callie raced over and adamantly asserted that her sister was wrong and had been an equal participant in their "game."

Grateful they'd temporarily diverted Monte's attention, Evie tried to think of a scenario that wouldn't make her appear irresponsible. Sadly, however she tried to spin it, she'd lost sight of the girls.

On her first day.

She'd be surprised if he didn't send her away before the night's end, and she wouldn't blame him one bit.

Chapter Four

"Sir, I'm really sorry—"

"No time for that now." This was not a great start to what he'd hoped would be a special, memory-making event. "Help me get the twins inside and cleaned up."

"Yes, sir." Taking Callie by the hand, Evie pivoted toward the front of the house.

"Not that way." He pointed to the back door.

The last thing he needed was for them to dirty the carpet.

He couldn't believe Evie had allowed this, especially so close to when he and the twins needed to leave. But he'd rather assume that than the alternative—that she'd left them unattended.

This felt like Tracy Gray all over again.

Clearly New Day Caregivers wasn't as wonderful as they claimed. One irresponsible employee, he could understand. He knew from working with numerous ranch hands over the years that people who seemed great during an interview could be the biggest dud of the bunch.

But two loafers in a row suggested a pattern.

At the entrance to the mudroom, he surveyed his property. Erin, his ex, now deceased, had taught him that not everyone considered this country setting a slice of heaven on earth.

What if the organization couldn't find competent staff willing to come out here? Sure, he could try another company, but then he'd have to begin the process all over. Making phone calls, asking questions, filling out forms and getting all the necessary medical documents transferred.

They'd probably stick him on a waiting list.

And who was to say another outfit would send him anyone better?

Evie and the girls followed him inside and stood in the center of the tan-and-cream tile while Monte warmed the water in the industrial-sized sink next to a row of boots. Above this hung a series of basket-filled cubbies.

Dropping to one knee, he shucked off Luna's outfit—the one she'd picked out specifically for today—and tossed it into a plastic hamper next to a large bag of dog food. The tears in her eyes tore at his heart.

Some might call him overly sensitive, reacting to her sorrow as he was. But he knew how excited she was for today's Christmas party, and to see her new school. He'd been hoping the event, and the opportunity to check out the facility for themselves, would ease his girls' first-day jitters. Late start or not, beginning preschool was a big deal.

Without a mama to see them off, that transition would be hard enough.

Jaw tight, he shot a glance at Evie as she tended to a chattering Callie. The child seemed intent on giving her version of events. As far as he could tell, Evie didn't know much more about the girls' mischief than he did.

Yet another indication that she'd left the twins unattended for a stretch of time.

Long enough for them to fill their plastic wading pool with enough dirt to plant a garden, add water and march around.

He wrapped his girls in stained towels to stop them from dripping water.

Throwing those into the hamper as well, he made eye contact with Evie. "You run a bath while I pick out their clothes."

She hurried to comply.

Grabbing a child under each arm, he followed. "All right, my little piggies. Time to leave the sty and return to the land of humans."

The girls giggled. Callie, the one who likely initiated their make-believe game, did so most enthusiastically.

He deposited the twins onto the pale blue linoleum where they waited for Evie to test the water and plug the tub.

"Can we have bubbles?" Callie's voice was sweet, as if she'd just come from cleaning up her toys without being asked, rather than swimming through mud.

Made sense considering she probably hadn't thought anything wrong with her fiasco, until she saw the adults' faces. Nor would she understand why Monte was so concerned.

Thank the good Lord for that. The last thing they needed was to feel untended to.

Regardless of how true that was.

"Everything all right?" Aunt Martha's voice, soft and kind, drifted from behind.

Evie looked up, tears pooling behind her long dark lashes. Torn between compassion for her obvious regret and frustration over all that had occurred, Monte took in a slow deep breath.

He explained what he'd found, upon returning to the house. With a full day booked, besides. While he'd happily made time for the party, his schedule didn't allow for an extensive cleanup. Or the fit Callie might throw when he tried to get her in yet another presentable outfit.

"Oh, my." His aunt laughed—her momentary amusement a gift in an otherwise unpleasant situation. "Can't take your eyes off them for a moment."

"That's a fact." He looked at Evie. "Which begs the question, how long were they out there, playing in the mud. And where, exactly, were you?"

She blinked rapidly, her gaze shooting from him to Aunt Martha, then back to him.

At least she wasn't firing off excuses. "This isn't a playground where you can let them do whatever they please."

"I know—"

"Do you? And if they'd been hurt while you were on social media or texting some guy, or doing whatever it was you were doing—other than what I'm paying you for. What then?"

The tears she'd fought back spilled over her lashes.

"Monte, that's enough." Aunt Martha spoke with more force than he'd heard from her in some time. She released a sigh, her shoulders and expression sagging. "She was helping me." Her entire body conveyed defeat.

He turned to Evie. "What happened?"

She looked at his aunt, as if seeking permission. When his aunt gave a slight nod, she told him about an incident he hadn't anticipated.

"Is this normal, getting dizzy like that?"

Evie shrugged. "It's not terribly uncommon. Could be a sign of dehydration or low blood sugar." She made eye contact with his aunt. "That's why it's so important that you do your best to eat."

Aunt Martha nodded again.

"It could also be from anemia, which can be a side effect of chemotherapy, or from anxiety and stress." Tub filled, Evie turned off the faucet.

Monte scrubbed a hand over his face, his irritation at finding his girls covered in mud replaced with deep gratitude for Evie's attentiveness with his aunt.

"I shouldn't have gotten so upset with you." He sighed. "The good Lord knows, those girls have landed in mudholes under my watch a time or two."

"Or ten?" Aunt Martha quirked an eyebrow at him.

He chuckled. "Or fifty-five. Thankfully, kids and clothes wash up well enough."

"But that was my favorite dress." Moisture pooled in Luna's eyes.

"And it was so beautiful." Evie smoothed the child's hair from her face. "In fact, I think it would be perfect for your first day of preschool. This will allow you to keep it a surprise while showing off one of the other dresses I saw in your closet. My favorite is the red one with the wide white bow. It's so Christmassy! Which do you like best, other than your first day of school surprise?"

Luna's face brightened. "I like the red one, too."

Evie clapped her hands together. "Wonderful! I can't wait to see it on you!"

Monte's heart warmed as he watched Evie interact with his daughter, and how the child's shyness began to melt away with her smile.

Maybe New Day had sent a more competent—and compassionate—caregiver than he'd thought.

"I want to wear my favorite clothes, too." Callie crossed her arms with a frown that warned him of an upcoming battle.

"So long as that means something without grass, food or dirt stains, sure." That about knocked out everything she considered comfortable. "Bonus points if it's red or green."

Spending the next thirty minutes sifting through her drawers would only leave them both frustrated. It'd probably trigger Callie's stubbornness as well, a trait he celebrated when it came to rodeoing, not so much when it complicated daily parenting.

"Anything I can do?" Aunt Martha asked.

He shook his head. "You go rest. With four hands for two girls, we've got them covered." He watched her leave, ready to accompany her if she seemed unsteady on her feet but unwilling to unnecessarily encroach on her independence.

Assured she was okay, he leaned toward Evie, inhaling her soft lavender scent. "You mention anything about taking them to the forest?"

She shook her head. The slight flush to her cheeks suggested she was as aware of his nearness as he was.

Clearing his throat, he widened the distance between them. "Tell you girls what." He lifted his daughters, one by one, into the tub. "How about I take you little explorers to your fort when we get back from meeting your teacher? May even catch us a glimpse of some deer or wild turkeys."

"Max and Ms. Evie, too?" Callie's eyes shimmered with hope.

"Doubt I could keep that dog from tromping around with you girls, even if I tried. As for Ms. Evie, if she wants. And isn't too upset about that fit I threw a moment ago."

She dropped her gaze and rubbed the back of her arm. Obviously, his invite had made her uncomfortable. She was probably searching for a polite way to decline.

He opened his mouth to save her the trouble when she offered the twins a wide smile. "That sounds fun."

He blinked. Not the answer he'd expected, and one that triggered much too intense a response within him.

Seemed he couldn't be near that woman without his palms turning sweaty. Last time he'd reacted that way around someone had been fifteen years ago, when he first met his ex. Although they attended the same high school, their paths hadn't crossed until his mom hired her to tutor him in biology.

He'd fallen for her hard and fast, and by the time they turned seniors, they were both dreaming about their future together. If only he'd known how quickly she'd bail, after they said their vows, he could've saved himself a whole lot of heartache.

But then they never would've had the twins. Those girls were well worth the grief their mama had caused.

His phone rang, and he glanced at the screen, then to Evie. "I need to grab this call." His friend wasn't one for chitchat, which meant, if he reached out, he had good reason.

"No problem."

With a nod, he slipped out, grateful for the excuse to distance himself from the woman whose pull on him only seemed to be getting stronger.

Considering his reaction after having spent less than forty-eight hours around her, he was increasingly uneasy regarding the next few weeks. And frustrated with himself for not doing better at keeping his emotions in check.

Midway through another ring, he answered. "Hey, Sean. What's up?"

His friend's sigh reverberated across the line. "It's Ian. He's acting up again, worse than ever. My sister and brother-in-law are at their wits' end. They don't want to give up on the kid, but nothing they've tried seems to work. My nephew's bent on destroying his life."

"Man, I'm sorry to hear that."

He ambled into the living room and paused to take in the scene. His kids had stretched a sheet from the coffee table over the back of the couch, and another from the table to the armchair, the edges anchored with their marble box, his Bible and a jar of coins. While not a fan of the mess, he did like to see that Evie allowed the children's creativity.

He picked up a sheet of paper. On it, one of the girls had drawn three stick figures, two smiling children standing on either side and holding the hands of an adult. Above this, they'd colored a heart.

While his girls would call about anyone a friend, it was nice to see the three of them getting along just the same.

"I'm hoping to find a positive outlet for my nephew to channel his energy into. Give him something to shoot for, know what I mean?"

"Makes sense. How can I help?"

"Actually…" Sean paused. "I was thinking it might be good to get him into bull riding. Think you can show him the ropes, maybe even let him help out on the ranch to compensate your time training him?"

"As to putting him to work, I'll have to think on that." Normally, Monte would welcome the opportunity to mentor a troubled teen, but that would require a good deal of supervision. With all he had going on, he wasn't sure he had the time or energy necessary for such an arrangement. "But I can coach him up, no problem. How about you bring him by Friday afternoon?"

"That'd be great. You have no idea how much I appreciate it."

"My pleasure." Ending the call, he scooped up an armful of stuffed animals and returned them to the girls' room.

Bath done, they met him there. Luna was already putting on her lace-trimmed red dress while Evie helped Callie sort through her clothes in search of something event-appropriate that didn't cause the child to scrunch up her face in overdramatized disgust.

"Isn't this adorable?" Evie pulled a short-sleeve dress from the closet with a denim top and green-and-white checked cotton from the waist down.

He leaned a shoulder against the doorframe. "That's cowpoke attire for sure."

Callie studied it with a furrowed brow that indicated her refusal would soon follow.

"Remember what I told you about taking you and your sister to the forest after." He glanced at the time on his phone. "If you cooperate. Which includes not spending the next thirty minutes fussing over what to wear."

Callie slumped. "Okay." She shrugged on the dress, making the process appear much more difficult than it could possibly be.

He grabbed a brush from on top of her dresser and secured her hair in a ponytail while Evie braided Luna's, upon her request. Ten minutes later, he was grabbing snacks for them to eat on the way and ushering them to the door.

Evie followed. "Sorry about the mess." She glanced back at the living room. "I'll clean up while you're gone."

Luna frowned. "You're not coming?"

His daughter only issued such requests to those she felt comfortable with. Had Evie managed to capture the child's heart already?

Biting her bottom lip, Evie looked at him, probably trying to gauge his preference.

The thought of her coming triggered a sense of anticipation that was almost a gut reaction—which in turn made him want her to stay home. Otherwise, he feared it wouldn't just be his children's hearts she'd capture.

"You know," Aunt Martha said from behind him, "might not be a bad idea for her to join y'all. I imagine she'll be helping the girls with their schoolwork and all and the one to pick them up, should they get sent home sick."

Monte rubbed the back of his neck. He fully intended to remain engaged in his daughters' education. He also disagreed that Evie needed to know their teacher to see they practiced their penmanship or studied their spelling words. But whenever his sweet Luna turned her big, brown eyes, brimming with hope, his way, he felt ready to give her the world.

"Okay." He gave her braid a gentle tug, then turned to Evie. "That is, if you're up for it."

She glanced again at the mess.

"Don't fret about that none." Aunt Martha flicked a hand. "This house has seen worse, believe me." She eyed Evie's muddied clothes. "Although you might want to change first."

Evie looked at Monte, as if seeking an invite.

"Go get yourself fixed up. We don't mind waiting." He

grabbed his car keys from a bowl on the entryway accent table. "As to all this—" he indicated the disheveled living room "—it'll still be here when you get back."

Evie laughed, a melodious sound that reminded him to keep a stronger rein on his emotions before they got away from him.

Chapter Five

Evie suspected Luna wasn't often quick to invite acquaintances into her world. Nor did Evie underestimate the importance of this event. She'd seen enough Instagram reels to realize that entering preschool was a huge transition. The girls probably were equally nervous and excited.

Most importantly, they wanted Evie to come. How could she possibly say no? Attending the party this afternoon would go a long way toward building trust, which was an important part of her job. Perhaps the most crucial, in fact. While it might appear the children had little say over her employment, she'd learned, a parent's heart was often deeply connected to their kids. As one of her friends often said, "You love my babies, I'll love you."

Plus, the Bowman girls were adorable. There were worse ways Evie could spend the afternoon.

She tossed Luna a smile. "I would love to come."

The child's bright-eyed grin squeezed her heart.

"Yay!" Callie jumped up and down, clapping. "You can see the playground. It's got two slides, swings, a jungle gym, and a rock wall. I climb up real fast." Her words trailed behind her as she skipped out of the house and down the stairs. "Daddy showed it to us after church last week. Said, with all the climbing we're bound to do, I'll get stronger and stronger." She flexed her nonexistent biceps.

Evie laughed. "I see." She looked up to find Monte watching her. When their eyes met, his gaze intensified, lingering on hers long enough to send a rush of heat to her face.

A man who, only moments ago, had seemed ready to give her the boot, and who still could, should another mud incident arise. Which wasn't unlikely, considering the setting.

With a deep breath, she tucked a lock of hair behind her ear and followed him out and onto the porch. Callie waited at the bottom step and slipped her hand into Evie's, flooding her chest with warmth. That child was as precious as she was rambunctious.

Monte's pickup, a metallic green with an extended cab, was parked in the shade of his shed. He opened the rear, driver's-side door, and the girls clambered in and fastened themselves into their car seats.

He rounded the front as if intending to open Evie's door for her, but she beat him to it. She was having difficulty enough maintaining her professional focus without him doing anything to increase his charm.

His cedary-citrus scent that accompanied him when he slid behind the wheel wasn't helping.

Fastening her seat belt, she focused on a series of questions Callie was firing off rather than the handsome cowboy sitting less than two feet away. The child's inquiries barely lasted five minutes before the girls started singing embellished lyrics to "Rudolph the Red-Nosed Reindeer."

Normally, she probably would've sung along, but she felt self-conscious doing so in front of Monte.

An awkward silence followed.

"So…" He drummed his fingers on the steering wheel, his pause suggesting he was trying equally hard to think of a conversation starter. "What were some of your favorite Christmas traditions?"

"Hmm… That's a tough one. I have so many special memories." She gazed out her window, mentally sifting through over two decades of family celebrations. "Probably eating my great-grandmother's home-baked cookies. She always brought a massive tubful. Oatmeal Raisin. Chocolate Chip. Soft and lemony sugar cookies. I also looked forward to finding and decorating our Christmas tree."

"Y'all had live ones?"

She nodded. "The morning after Thanksgiving, we got all bundled up. Winters can be quite cold in Michigan."

"I imagine."

"Mom would fill a bunch of thermoses with hot cocoa. Then half of us would pile into my dad's truck, the other half followed in our station wagon. We'd head to a family-owned farm outside of town to find the best Christmas tree possible, not that any of us agreed upon which one that was."

He laughed. "Y'all did a bit of bickering, I take it?"

She nodded. "Which usually ended in a brutal—and fun—snowball fight. Initiated by my dad."

"That's one way to redirect squabbling siblings."

She angled her head. "Huh. I never thought of it that way, before. My dad was such a sneak!" She grinned, more impressed with her father's gentle parenting than ever. "What about you?"

On their right, two women in jeans and sweatshirts power-walked side by side. Beyond them, a man hung lights from his gutters while a woman and two teenagers decorated the porch and bordering bushes. A golden retriever supervised from where he lay in the yard.

"I've got to copy your cookies answer." Monte shot her a grin that halted her breath. "The ladies usually baked them together while we guys watched football and pestered them for spoonfuls of dough. I loved the smell of melted chocolate and vanilla that swirled throughout my grandparents' house."

His memories were allowing her to see a different, more

nostalgic side of him that she found endearing. For that reason alone, she'd be wise to shift to another topic. But her curiosity, tinged with a growing fondness, won out. "What was the best gift you ever received?"

"A twenty-piece electric train set."

"You answered that quickly. Must've been quite the toy."

He nodded. "It was actually for both my brother and me. Because of how expensive it was. Not that my parents were poor or anything. But they were always careful to keep the main thing the main thing."

"Jesus?"

He nodded. "Like they reminded us a thousand times, it was His birthday, after all. In Christ, God the Father had already given us the best gift possible. They never wanted us to forget that."

"I respect that."

"I didn't always like their logic back then, but I appreciate it now. I want to raise my girls the same way—to value faith and family more than some fancy gadget that they'll lose, break or grow bored of."

"They're blessed to have you."

He chuckled. "Doubt they'll feel that way once they hit the teen years. You know what they say about parenting?"

"It's a long game?"

He gave a slight shrug. "Isn't that the truth. But what I was going to say was if your kids aren't upset with you about something, you're doing it wrong."

"Ah. So, if you come home to find the kids pitching a fit, you'll recognize that as a sign of my competency?" Their easy banter had eradicated the insecurity with which she'd climbed into his vehicle. That felt like a dangerous shift, considering how appealing she found the man, and more so with every encounter.

He turned onto a residential street lined with numerous

houses that clearly went all out for the holidays. One had a large wooden display of Santa in a sleigh overflowing with brightly painted boxes. Another had decorated the massive tree anchoring their lawn with fake candy canes.

But had the town held a competition, the prize would've gone to the homeowners two blocks down. Their yard looked like a winter wonderland, with a snowflake-adorned multi-sectioned archway stretching the length of their walk, and giant lollipops staked in the grass.

They passed the local high school, another short stretch of houses, then turned into a small circular lot filled with about a dozen other vehicles. The brightly painted sign on the single-story building said Bright Start Preschool. Someone had painted large ornaments with silver tops and holly with bright red berries on the windows. But she most loved their nativity scene, with Mary and Joseph kneeling on either side of baby Jesus's manger.

"Here we are." He parked next to a station wagon with plastic taped over a partially busted rear window and cut the engine. "Your new school." He flashed his daughters a smile. "Big girls only."

Evie slipped out, opened Luna's door and helped her climb from the truck. Apparently, she'd increased her connection with the child, because, although not as exuberantly affectionate as her sister, she remained at Evie's side as they strode toward the entrance. Callie, on the other hand, raced ahead, then back, then up ahead again before hanging by her knees from a bike rack.

Reaching her, Monte tickled her ribs, scooped her up and dangled her, laughing, over his shoulder. "Come on, little monkey."

Once inside, he placed her on her feet, catching her by the arm before she darted ahead once again.

"Hold on, Cowpoke. Let's find out where we need to go before you go blazing off and wind up in the custodial closet."

Callie angled her head, brow furrowed. "What's that?"

"Lots of scrubbing, sweeping and mopping, that's what."

Evie laughed. "You're great at positive redirection." Had he answered the child any other way, she probably would've been more determined than ever to go exploring.

He grinned. "Kinda have to be, raising that fireball on a bucking bull ranch and all."

His statement reminded her of the challenge that lay ahead. Keeping that girl out of mud-filled pools was the least of her concerns.

"Well, look who we have here." A tall, lanky woman with curly gray hair approached with a wide smile. She wore a sweatshirt with a decorated tree on it and a lanyard bearing her name and the phrase I Can Help.

"Mrs. Gutierre!" Callie ran toward her with her arms outstretched.

Laughing, the woman dropped to one knee and pulled the child into a firm embrace.

"Ma'am." Monte tipped his hat. "I didn't realize you worked here." As she stood, he introduced her and Evie to one another.

"I don't. Just volunteering." Stepping forward, Mrs. Gutierre drew Luna into a hug then took Evie's hands in hers and gave a gentle squeeze. "It's so nice to meet you."

"Mrs. Gutierre volunteers in children's ministry one Sunday a month," Monte said. "As you can tell, the kids love her, mine included."

"And I them." The woman turned her warm, kind eyes to Evie. "Thank you for taking care of our sweet Martha. As you probably know, this town would be devastated without her."

These types of conversations were as touching as they were stressful. Evie loved seeing the legacy of a life lived well, evident in the depth of relationships formed. And yet, hearing such adoration also served as a reminder of how many people were placing their hopes not just in Aunt Martha's treatment, but in Evie's caregiving abilities as well. Logically, most understood there was only so much she could do. The real battle lay with the doctors, the chemotherapy and Martha's strength to fight.

But in these situations, the heart often disregarded the head and people grasped on to every bit of hope possible.

The adults engaged in conversation a moment longer, but then Callie became restless and began pulling on her father's arm, urging him forward.

"Patience, Cowpoke." The amused glint in his eyes contradicted his stern tone. "You'll have plenty of time in this building, believe me." With a chuckle, he took a flyer Mrs. Gutierre offered, glanced at it, then used it to bop Luna on the head. "Ready, kiddo?"

Face bright with wonder and a hint of anxiety, she nodded.

Together, they followed brightly colored, hand-drawn signs past a gym/cafeteria, around the corner, and to the last classroom on the left. The melody to "Frosty the Snowman" and the sound of voices floated toward them.

Inside, Ms. Vargas, the pre-K teacher, greeted them. About thirty years younger than Mrs. Gutierre, she had blond hair, green eyes and a petite frame well suited for her forest green cotton dress. She wore ornament earrings and a light-up Christmas necklace.

Monte introduced her to Evie. "Kate here attends Trinity Faith. We've known each other for at least fifteen years, wouldn't you say?"

The teacher nodded. "Ever since Drake's younger sister Elizabeth started inviting me to youth group. Back when I had a crush on his best friend." Her laughter indicated she was referring to Monte.

His slight blush confirmed that. "A long time, that's for sure."

Why did their warm familiarity prick Evie with a twinge of jealousy? So what that he had a pretty friend—and the two didn't seem any more than that. It wasn't like Evie had any claim on the man, or that she'd stick around long enough to change that.

However, her reaction did increase her desire to get into nursing school and get hired on at a local hospital. One in a city with a thriving art and music culture, great restaurants and opportunities to meet someone and fall in love.

God willing, someone with the strength, kindness and integrity she detected in Monte.

Hand resting on his belt buckle, he surveyed the classroom. "Quite the setup you've got here."

Empty cubbies stood along the wall between them and a corner reading nook designated by a tiered book display. Beanbags and a mural of a tree house occupied the corner. Square tables, each with four chairs arranged around them, and colorful plastic caddies filled with various craft supplies were arranged in the center. On the far wall hung a decorated bulletin board, a window to its right, bins of blocks and other manipulatives to its left.

"I like to provide the children with ample opportunities to engage their curiosity." Ms. Vargas began explaining some of the sensory stations placed about the room. "They learn best through play and a sense of wonder."

"Impressive," Monte said. "The girls will think every day's a party here. After seeing all this, they'll be biting at the bit for their first day."

Ms. Vargas grinned. "Then I've accomplished my goal."

To Evie's left stood a do-it-yourself photo booth type of display designated with a fake fir adorned in ornaments and tinsel, a yellow bench and a framed chalkboard with the words *Merry Christmas* in bold lettering.

"Girls, look." She pointed. "Let me take some photos for your aunt Martha."

Luna's eyes brightened. Callie slumped but complied with minimal coaxing.

Evie snapped a picture of each child by herself, with one another, and then their dad.

"Can I take one with you, too?" Luna asked.

Evie's heart melted. "Absolutely." But the warmth the child's request brought turned to nervousness once she was standing behind the twins, shoulder to shoulder with Monte.

As if she were part of their family.

Thank goodness, Callie's impatience broke the moment before it became too awkward.

"Daddy?" She tugged on her father's arm. "Can I go paint?" She pointed to a series of standing easels where two other children had gathered.

Monte looked at Ms. Vargas, who turned to his daughter with a warm smile. "Absolutely."

"Yay!" Callie skipped off and introduced herself to a round-bellied, chubby-cheeked boy with spiked black hair and a red-headed girl in a turquoise T-shirt and rainbow-print skorts.

While Ms. Vargas described various activities she'd planned for her students during the months ahead, Luna lingered between Evie and her dad. Her gaze locked on a lady and her child working a puzzle set up in one of the corners.

"Is this open play time?" Evie asked.

Ms. Vargas glanced at the clock on the wall above her. "For about fifteen more minutes, yes."

Evie made eye contact with Luna. "Shall we go join them at the puzzle table?"

The child's eyes widened for a flash of a second, then she gave a weak shrug.

Poor girl wanted to make friends. She just needed someone to help her gain the courage.

"Come on." Evie took the child's hand in hers and guided her across the room to where the mother and her daughter sat around a circular table covered with colorful puzzle pieces. "Mind if we join you?"

The mom looked up, her eyes warm and friendly. "Not at all." She stood and initiated a handshake. "I'm Brooke, and this is my youngest, Destiny." She motioned to her daughter. "I also have a third and fifth grader. They're at home playing video games with their dad."

Based on the way Destiny leaned into her mom, as if wanting to hide behind her, she was about shy as Luna. That could make them a great match.

Or lead to awkward silence.

Choosing a navy chair short enough to bring her knees to her ears, Evie introduced herself and Luna. "I bet you both have a lot in common." She tried to think of something that would help the girls connect. "Do you like animals?"

Sitting a tad straighter, Destiny nodded. "I've got a dog named Big Bear."

"What about you, Luna?" Brooke found a corner puzzle piece and snapped it into place. "Do you have any pets?"

She nodded. "Two dogs. Max and Finn." Her voice was soft.

After a few more gentle proddings, the girls relaxed and soon meandered over to a dress-up area on the other side of a colorful rug, leaving Evie and Brooke to complete the puzzle.

"Do you have other children?" the woman asked.

"Oh, no. The twins aren't mine." She explained her relationship to them.

"The Bowman ranch?"

She nodded.

"That must be hard."

"It can be. But my job can also be deeply fulfilling. It feels good to know I'm making a positive impact on someone."

"No, I mean living out there and seeing what those poor animals are forced to endure." She shook her head.

Evie frowned. "I don't know what you mean, or what it's like on other ranches. But from what I can see, Mr. Bowman treats his animals well."

"You've never watched them buck, I take it?" The woman went on to tell her about a flank strap she felt certain caused the bulls pain. "No offense, but it makes me ill to think about it. Can't understand the type of man that would subject a creature to such torment."

Jaw slack, Evie looked at Monte, who'd moved to the easel area and was squatting down, eye level with Callie.

Was what Brooke said true? From what she'd observed, that seemed hard to believe, although she had seen a hint of a temper during the mud incident. At the time, she hadn't thought his reaction extreme. Not to mention, he really seemed to love his bulls, and his girls.

Then again, she didn't know Monte well, nor would she stick around long enough to change that. In the meantime, common sense told her to disregard any and all small-town gossip, which was what this felt like.

Still, her inner caretaker couldn't help but bristle at the idea that Monte's personality carried even a hint of cruelty.

Monte glanced up to see Evie talking with Brooke Sanders and frowned. Terrific. He could only imagine the type of garbage that busybody was spewing. So convinced he was a heartless rancher, she'd made it her mission to harass and badmouth him every chance she got.

Regardless that her perspective was skewed, her falsehoods were perpetuated by animal rights groups and those who were clueless when it came to raising rough stock. Had Mrs. Meddle taken the time to check her assumptions, he would've kindly set her straight. Even given her a tour of his ranch. But then she'd have to find some other way to satisfy her self-righteous hunger for superiority.

Evie, he hoped, had enough wisdom to disregard, or at least question, the woman's prattle.

Refocusing on Kate, who was in the middle of explaining her online communication system, he waited for her to pause. "Would you excuse me for a moment?"

"Yes, of course."

Why was he concerned with what Evie thought, anyway? It wasn't like they had, or ever would have, anything other than a working relationship.

Although their interactions would be much more pleasant if she didn't think of him as a callous jerk.

Both women glanced up as he approached. "Ma'am." He greeted Brooke with a tip of his hat. "Is Destiny excited about starting school?" Some guys might try to avoid their enemies. He figured his display of human dignity was one of the best ways to expose her immaturity.

Expression hard, Brooke gave a shrug that almost resembled a twitch. "She's always been an enthusiastic reader."

He expected her to use the opportunity to brag about her daughter. Instead, she turned to Evie with a stiff smile. "It was nice meeting you. And if you'd like more information on my book club, don't hesitate to give me a call."

Great. The two had exchanged numbers.

Suppressing a huff, he eyed the partially completed puzzle spread across the table, then glanced at Callie. She and two other children were playing with an educational display made from cords, clothespins and various circle cutouts.

"Can't imagine my little cowpoke will find anything boring about this place."

Evie nodded. "Your friend has created an inviting environment, that's for sure. And apparently, she can turn almost any lesson into a game."

"I'm not surprised. Kate's always been creative. Here I've been fretting about getting Callie to school without a fuss each morning. Now I'm thinking I'll have a tough time enticing her to come home."

"Well, there's always Max."

"True that. And Aunt Martha. Doubt either of them could stay away from her long."

Evie dropped her gaze with a hint of a frown.

"All right, everyone." Now standing in the center of the room, Ms. Vargas clapped her hands. "How about a fun game of pin the carrot on the snowman?"

The children cheered and hurried over, Callie among the first in line. Luna, not surprisingly, hung back. For a moment, he feared she wouldn't participate. But then Brooke's daughter took her hand and said, "Come on."

While not exactly thrilled by her choice of a playmate, he was thankful that she had found a friend. Besides, it wouldn't be right to judge a child based on her mother's behavior.

After three more games and cookie decorating, Ms. Vargas released the children to once again engage in whatever activities they pleased. Callie joined a group of boys playing with tractors and dump trucks while Luna and her new friend gravitated toward the dress-up area again.

Feeling a bit out of place as the only father in the room, Monte lingered near the door, reading through his emails.

"Daddy!" Callie hurried over with bright eyes, a newfound friend at her side, followed by a woman he vaguely remembered from one of the story time gatherings at the library. "Can I go to Bobby's house to play? His mama said it's okay."

He assumed she was referring to the boy with short brown hair standing beside her. "Hello." He shook hands with the child's mother. "I'm Monte."

"Abigail." She pulled her son's index and middle fingers from his mouth and turned to Evie. "Seems our kiddos hit it off. I'm part of our local moms' club. We get together for park days and playdates. This afternoon, I'm hosting a get-together at my house. You and your daughters are welcome to join us." She glanced Luna's way. "Callie mentioned her twin."

Evie blinked, apparently taken aback. "Oh, I'm not her mother. I'm their aunt's caregiver."

"Cancer," Monte said.

Sympathy lines stretched across Abigail's forehead. "I'm so sorry. I know that can be quite the battle."

"I appreciate that."

"Can I go?" Callie clenched folded hands beneath her chin. "I'll be real good and will mind my manners and not talk too much or interrupt. Or jump on their couch, either."

Her enthusiasm made him smile. "Really, now? Those are some mighty big promises." He bopped her on the nose.

"But I mean it."

He rubbed the back of his neck, thinking through the rest of his day. He wasn't keen on sending his girls off with a woman he didn't know, nor of Evie accompanying them. They'd left Aunt Martha untended long enough. Plus, he still had a lot to take care of, back at the ranch.

"Another day, Cowpoke."

She groaned with an overdramatic slump. "How come?"

He explained and looked at the time on his phone. "Speaking of, we best round up your sister if y'all want to hit the playground before we leave."

Her frown indicated she didn't consider this a fair trade, although her mood lightened considerably when he reminded her about playing in the creek later.

On the drive home, however, she was uncharacteristically quiet.

He glanced at her through the rearview mirror to find her staring out her window. "You all right back there?"

She didn't respond right away, then she released a heavy sigh. "I want a mama like everyone else."

His chest squeezed, and his throat turned tight and scratchy.

Lucy had warned him events like this could remind the girls of what they didn't have. Told him to think about how he might answer their hard questions. But no words, no matter how logical, could ease his little girl's ache.

"I know." His near whisper came out hoarse.

He wanted that for them, too.

Chapter Six

❧

The doctor was at the house when they returned. Seeing his gray station wagon sitting near the shed tightened Monte's muscles with a burst of adrenaline. Had Aunt Martha fallen again? He never should've taken Evie with him and the girls to that Christmas party, especially after her dizzy spell this morning.

What had he been thinking?

Clearly, he hadn't been.

Parking a foot from the porch steps, he looked at Evie. "See to the girls?"

She nodded, her wrinkled brow indicating she sensed his concern. "Everything all right?"

He glanced at his daughters to find their big eyes trained on him. "Yep."

The twins tended to take their emotional cues from him. If he acted all worked up, they'd become frightened. One of the best ways to teach his girls how to have faith was to keep it himself.

Seemed that was all he'd been clinging to, of late.

Stepping out of the truck, he pocketed his keys and ascended the steps two at a time. The front door and screen stood propped open, the interior dim compared to the afternoon sun.

"Aunt Martha?" As he hurried toward her bedroom, a splash of color filled his peripheral vision, along with quiet voices. With a deep inhale, he stopped and turned back around.

Doc Tackett met Monte in the archway separating the living room and kitchen. "Howdy." He wore jeans and a blue, collared shirt.

Aunt Martha sat at the table behind him, looking tired but less so than before her fall. Less discouraged, too.

"Doc. Thanks for coming." He shook the man's hand, then went to his aunt. "You feeling better?"

"Much." She smiled. "The party go well?"

By now Evie and the girls had joined them, and Callie began telling her about pert near every detail of her classroom.

"I made a friend." The child grinned. "We both like climbing trees, catching lizards and making mud pies."

Remembering their morning fiasco, he stole a glance at Evie and was captivated by the soft blush on her cheeks.

Clearing his throat and his head, he turned back to the doctor. "We weren't expecting you until tomorrow."

Doc gave a one-shoulder shrug. "My schedule freed up unexpectedly today. Made plans to go skeet shooting with a buddy of mine that lives one county over. Figured I'd stop in here on the way."

Apparently, this reminded Callie of Monte's promise to take her and her sister to the woods, because she abandoned the story she'd been telling Aunt Martha and dragged her sister off with her to change into playclothes.

Monte slipped a hand into his pocket. "Everything check out?"

Doc looked at Aunt Martha, and his eyes softened. "Don't know yet what her blood work shows, obviously. But considering her numbers last week and her fall this morning…" Straightening, he shifted to face Monte. "She's asked to cancel this week's treatment, and I'm inclined to agree. Give her time to grow stronger."

Monte scrubbed a hand over his face. "Okay." Every delay felt like a setback. While he knew logically her cancer wasn't likely to spread due to a one-week layoff, it didn't alleviate his anxiety any.

Then again, he doubted anything would until he heard the words they were fighting toward—remission.

The doctor gathered his things. "In the meantime, I encourage you to eat foods that naturally help increase blood platelets. Spinach. Broccoli. The Literary Sweet Spot's got a tasty papaya smoothie. With just enough fresh fruit to make the ice cream base healthy."

Aunt Martha sighed. "For a small fortune, I'm sure."

"May do you good to get out of the house now and again." The doctor leveled his gaze on her, then turned to Evie. "On another note, welcome to Sage Creek. I hear you won't be staying long." He made eye contact with Monte. "Make sure she tries a piece of the Herrings' fresh peach cobbler before she leaves."

"Will do." He walked him to the door, his aunt and Evie following. "We really appreciate you stopping by. We know how busy you are. Nurse Geneva out on maternity yet?"

"As of last week, yep. And it sounds like she's not planning on coming back, least not for a few years."

Aunt Martha gave a compassionate shake of her head. "Sorry to hear it. I know how challenging it can be to find compassionate and competent help."

"'Spect you do."

Wasn't that the truth. As far as Monte knew, New Day still hadn't found Evie's replacement. They never came right out and said that, but they hadn't sent him any information on anyone, either. Although, considering what had happened with Ms. Gray, they probably were being extra cautious.

He appreciated that—so long as they sent him someone by the time Evie was fixing to leave.

Monte waited until the doctor got into his car. With a last wave, he stepped back inside and closed the door. He studied his aunt, struck by how much she'd aged over the past few months. Course, it didn't help how little she was eating.

"You up for a smoothie?" He eyed the browning bananas in the fruit bowl, then faced Evie. "We've got strawberries and blackberries in the freezer. Enough for her and the girls. They'll want a frozen treat, too. But we'll probably need more for the days ahead. If I write you a list, can you hit the grocery store when you get a chance?"

"Absolutely."

By now, the girls had returned dressed in playclothes. As usual, Callie had her butterfly net that she used to catch lizards, frogs and whatever other creepy-crawlies she could find. She'd probably snag the small red cooler still sitting by the porch stairs where she'd last left it. Noting Luna's tote, likely filled with at least one book, he was struck once again by how different those two were.

He expected they'd both start out in their fort, which he'd helped them build in an alcove of trees. That was the only time they'd allowed him near their "secret, girls-only" hideaway. Inevitably, Callie would grow bored of their imaginary play and become engrossed in building a "critter habitat" of sorts from sticks, stones, mud and straw. Meanwhile, her sister would find a smooth rock to sit upon and flip through one of the illustrated nature books borrowed from the library.

"Are you coming, too?" Callie looked up at Aunt Martha with hope-filled eyes.

He could tell she was struggling to respond, probably feeling the same ache he did at how much had changed. But only for a season.

He placed a hand on his daughter's shoulder. "Not today, Cowpoke. Your aunt needs to rest."

"She can rest there, and read books with Luna, like she used to."

"Another time."

Callie's frown deepened. "All she does is sleep. She never does anything fun anymore." She dropped her net on the floor and stormed down the hallway.

Monte wasn't sure what tore at his heart more, seeing his daughter's pain and obvious longing for how things used to be, or the defeated look on his aunt's face.

He reached for her hand and gave it a gentle squeeze. "She'll be all right."

Aunt Martha offered a slight nod.

In situations like this, he wished his kids had a mama to help them process, because he hadn't a clue how to respond. He couldn't make sense of his own emotions half the time.

"Do you mind if I talk with her?" Evie asked.

He released a breath. She must've sensed his inner angst, evident by the fact that his feet remained planted.

He shrugged. "You probably have more experience with these types of things than I do." True, she hadn't worked with kids much, but she'd probably been trained in what to say, or not to say to family members with loved ones fighting cancer.

"I don't know about that, but I have been told I give a mean hug." As if to prove this, she wrapped an arm around Luna, who stood in the center of the kitchen, taking it all in, and pulled her close. Worried expression smoothing into a hint of a smile, the child leaned into her.

He quirked an eyebrow, grateful for the lightened mood. "Mean hug. Isn't that an oxymoron?"

She laughed, a gentle, melodious sound. "Touché."

He watched her leave, his other daughter trailing after her, then turned to his aunt. "Mind if I add one of those protein shakes I bought into your smoothie?"

"That's fine." Her tone indicated she didn't have much of an appetite.

Knowing Evie might be occupied with Callie for a while,

he pulled his aunt's food processor from the cupboard and added enough ingredients to fill three glasses.

The whir of the machine mirrored the anxious thoughts swirling through his brain. He'd known going into it that his aunt's battle against cancer would be tough, but he'd not expected the emotional weight of all the unknowns.

His aunt had to feel discouraged. Hearing the doc recommend delaying treatment would've been difficult enough. Then to think her very fight for life was inflicting pain upon the girls she adored more than anything.

They could all use a pick-me-up. Matter of fact, a bit of fresh air would do his aunt good. She had always loved spending time with the twins at the creek. It was a lovely December day. The sky was clear, the sun was out. If only the walk there wasn't so long.

He brightened. She could drive the Side-by-Side. Why hadn't he thought of that sooner?

Feeling like he was about to give Callie a new set of boots, he placed his aunt's drink on the table in front of her, kissed her temple, then hurried to his daughter's room.

The image that greeted him squeezed his chest. Evie sat on the floor, legs stretched in front of her, a twin under each arm. She rested her chin on Callie's head while, on her other side, Luna nestled in close.

"What do you love most about going to the forest with your aunt?"

Callie grinned. "Showing her all my tricks. I can climb trees and hang upside down by my knees, with no hands. She says I'm like a little monkey." She turned serious. "That means strong and fast."

"It feels good to know she's proud of you, doesn't it?"

Callie nodded.

Evie glanced down at Luna and smoothed the hair from her face. "And what do you love most?"

"When she reads to me."

It was probably because of his aunt that his daughter loved books so much. For the same reason Callie enjoyed "showing off." Aunt Martha had a way of making them all feel like they were the most important people in the world.

They felt the same about her.

"Is there another way you can make her proud of you?" Evie asked.

Monte stepped into the room. "Y'all could put on one of your shows for her."

"Yeah!" Callie sprang to her feet. "Like the *Three Little Bears*. Or *Santa Lost His Reindeer*." She continued listing other titles. "Can we have real curtains, like Ms. Vargas's?"

He liked hearing her speak so positively about their classroom. That and their pleasant experience that afternoon should help eliminate any first-day anxiety tears.

He and Evie exchanged an amused smile that felt far too intimate. He was touched to see how much she seemed to genuinely enjoy his girls. Then again, that was her job. She wouldn't be that great a caregiver if she didn't actually care.

Then again, Ms. Gray had played the part and had fooled them all.

But she'd never looked at the twins—or himself—the way Evie did.

What was he doing? He had no business thinking this way, and especially not about someone he'd soon never see again.

Cheeks flushed, he cleared his throat and began tossing stray toys into their bin.

Once certain his blush no longer showed, he told the girls about his forest solution.

"Yay!" Callie once again began skipping around the room, her mouth moving faster than her feet. Calling out to his aunt, the child rushed out with her sister following close behind.

Evie stood. "I'd say that just won you Father of the Year award."

"Maybe if I'd thought of that before the drama…" He laughed to hide the smile her kind words and the note of admiration in her voice triggered.

Considering how he reacted when the woman offered even a hint of a compliment, he'd be wise to limit their time together. Yet, here he was, about to spend the afternoon with her at the creek.

He hoped the girls would provide enough of a distraction to keep him from thinking about things he had no business entertaining.

Like the way Evie's face brightened whenever one of the girls engaged her in conversation. Or how her head tilted ever so slightly when Callie did something silly. Or the way her eyes softened when she looked at his aunt, or seemed to intensify when they shifted in his direction.

As if he intrigued her.

A ridiculous thought. If anything, she was trying to figure him out and what he wanted. He was sort of her boss, after all.

And she was here to save his aunt's life, which was what he needed to focus on.

Outside, Evie and the others waited on the porch while Monte trotted off to get his ATV. Apparently, he'd left it out by the arena. Callie used the slight delay to alternate between jumping off the bottom step and playing fetch with Max. Luna lingered between her and her aunt, glancing from one to the other, before climbing into her aunt's lap.

Had she been contemplating sitting with Evie? The thought caused her heart to swell. Prior to coming here, she'd felt certain kids weren't her thing.

Granted, she was far from an expert—and still had to make it through her end date without the girls experiencing anything catastrophic. She was finding her time here on the ranch much more pleasant than expected.

Unfortunately, she was finding her interactions with Monte more enjoyable than anticipated, or helpful, as well.

Now she had a new concern. Were the twins becoming too attached to her? She didn't want to set them up for a hard goodbye.

The low rumble of an engine caught her attention. She turned to see Xavier approach in a swirl of dust. Grinning, he stopped in front of the porch, a disarming combination of boyish playfulness and rugged cowboy.

Her breath stalled as an image flashed through her mind of the two of them horse riding across his property, him in front, her arms wrapped around his middle, her cheek pressed to his back.

He had much too strong an effect on her.

This forest adventure was a bad idea.

"I can manage the girls while you take care of whatever you need to on the ranch." The breeze stirred a lock of hair in front of her eye. She swept it away. "I'll text you with any concerns."

He gazed down the dirt road leading to the far side of his property and scratched his jaw. Seemed he didn't want to come any more than she wanted him to, although likely for a vastly different reason. He had a ranch to run, after all, not act as caregiver.

That was why he'd hired her.

On a temporary basis, after which she'd never see him, his aunt or the adorable twins ever again.

The fact that this disappointed her only amplified her concerns regarding this little outing.

He pulled his phone and looked at the screen. "I do need to fix a leak in the hay barn and should probably ride the fence." Her confusion must have shown on her face because he added, "Check for places in need of repair."

She nodded, relieved and disappointed by his response.

And much too pleased when the girls' pleading changed his mind.

Mercy, she was a mess.

He swung a leg over to dismount his vehicle and climbed the porch steps in long, easy strides. "You ready, Aunt Martha?" He reached out a hand to help her rise then walked beside her, to the ATV-like vehicle he referred to as a Side-by-Side.

Evie and the girls followed and lingered, the dogs nearby, as Aunt Martha got settled on the vehicle.

"The dust won't bother you?" Monte asked.

Evie was once again struck by the tenderness he showed his loved ones. But what about his animals? Was what that woman from the party said true?

Granted, she'd seen how kind he'd been to his horses and dogs. Did he treat his bulls differently? How'd he get them to buck, anyway?

How he ran his ranch shouldn't matter, nor would it affect how she did her job. It could, however, temper her attraction to the man.

Compassion for his animals aside, that would be a good thing.

Chapter Seven

The next morning, Monte followed the scent of cooked bacon and buttery flour into the kitchen. Seemed Evie was already making use of the groceries she'd picked up the evening before.

He paused before entering to smooth his hair, then chastised himself for it—along with the slight spike in his pulse at the thought of encountering Evie.

The woman was his aunt's caregiver, nothing more. Maybe if he told himself that enough, logic would overpower his growing affection toward her.

With a sigh, he turned and stepped into the room, mentally processing the image of his aunt standing at the stove. With her normally slumped shoulders squared, she almost appeared like her formerly strong self.

She glanced at him with a genuine smile. "Morning."

He greeted her with a kiss on the cheek. "You're looking bright-eyed and bushy-tailed. Does this mean you're feeling better?"

"I'm looking forward to a week free of nausea."

He admired her positive outlook, but also worried she might be acting braver than she felt. She had to be frustrated by her delayed treatment, but probably didn't want to increase his anxiety. She always put others first.

Regardless, the delay was temporary—so she could grow stronger.

Doc's advice carried weight. He was as knowledgeable as he was trustworthy, and he loved Aunt Martha near as much as Monte and the girls.

He poured himself a mug of fresh-brewed coffee. The rich aroma soothed him. "The girls still asleep?"

Aunt Martha chuckled. "Oh, my, no. Callie and Luna were up by five thirty and whisked Evie off to help them gather chicken eggs."

"Impressive." And yet one more indication of how much they'd taken to Evie.

As if on cue, the front door clanked open, and enthusiastic voices drifted toward him. The twins and Evie appeared a moment later, the latter carrying a basket half-filled with eggs.

Evie's eyes danced with laughter, as if spending time with the girls brought her joy. She wore her hair down, and he felt an unexpected urge to run his hands through her soft, silky waves.

With a mental shake, he greeted her with a nod he hoped didn't appear rude or awkward and focused on his daughters. "What kind of mischief have y'all been up to this morning?"

Not surprisingly, Luna was already dressed in the newly cleaned—and stain-free—outfit her sister had splattered with mud the day before. Callie, on the other hand, remained in pajamas, which now had bits of straw attached to them.

Frowning, his daughter stomped to the stove. "You didn't wait for the eggs."

Aunt Martha placed steaming bacon onto a paper-towel-covered plate. "Y'all told me you didn't want any this morning, remember? So that you could save tummy space for pancakes."

"I changed my mind."

His aunt placed a hand on Callie's head. "Then this'll be a great lesson on following through on what you say."

Seeing how his daughter was already disappointed, Monte figured it'd be a good time to tell her to change into her school clothes. As expected, she slumped with one of her melodramatic moans but complied.

Shaking her head, his aunt set food on the table. "Someone should sign that child up for acting club. If you can keep her off a bull long enough to get her on the stage."

He laughed. "Now, that would be the challenge of the century." The way Evie was watching him indicated she wanted to say something, so he invited her to do so.

She still seemed hesitant.

"Come on now," he said. "Spit it out."

She placed a pitcher of orange juice on the table. "Are you worried she'll take your statements seriously and wind up bull riding when she gets older?"

He pulled a stack of plates from the cupboard and distributed them at each place setting. "You saying her rodeoing would be a bad thing?"

She lowered her gaze. "I misunderstood. I apologize."

"If you think bull riding is too dangerous for my girls, I'd say so's felling trees, fighting fires and chasing criminals. I wouldn't deter the twins from working in any of those fields. I'd rather teach them to follow their heart, and the good Lord, wherever He leads, than to live enslaved to fear. Or to think that some things are off-limits to females."

"I meant no offense."

"None taken." Her question had been harmless enough. But he'd known what she'd been thinking. Why had her statement gotten him so riled up? It wasn't like he hadn't heard others convey similar thoughts.

However, her comment *did* remind him of why, if he fell in love again, it would be with a woman who loved the country. That was one lesson Erin had taught him well.

Yet, no one had ever directed their statements at his girls, which by association meant at him as a dad. That was an area in which he often felt he failed, especially since his aunt had become sick.

Regardless, he wouldn't raise his girls to believe they weren't fit for certain careers, or to feel compelled to prove their value as females. He'd seen enough cowgirls to know that could lead to reckless behavior more dangerous than getting into the bucking chute.

Besides, he wouldn't act a hypocrite by directing them from an industry in which he invested most of his waking hours.

He sipped his coffee. "I trust so long as I teach them to seek God, when they need to make those types of decisions, He'll show them where and when to step."

"Yes, of course." Poor woman looked like she'd been sent to the feed lot.

He was about to ease the tension invading the room when the twins burst back in, Callie asking about bringing her "laundry rocks" to school.

Evie looked from one person to the next with raised eyebrows. "Laundry rocks?"

Monte chuckled. "Crumpled pieces of paper she sticks in her pocket that get run through the wash. Come out hard and small like pebbles from the driveway."

"I see."

Aunt Martha placed a stack of pancakes in the center of the table and sat. "The first time was an accident. But she liked the results so much, she's been doing it ever since."

"Good info." Evie looked at the child with as much seriousness as if they'd been discussing precious stones. "When I do laundry, I'll make sure to leave your treasures be."

Grinning, Callie climbed into the chair beside her and revealed small, compacted wads in her palm. This led to a discussion on show and tell, an activity that excited both girls. He hoped that would counter any first-day anxiety that could otherwise make it challenging to get them off to school.

"You know, you and the girls should add something fun and relaxing to your to-do list," Aunt Martha said. "I'm sure Evie would love to experience some of the perks to ranching life." She looked at Evie. "It isn't all mucking stalls and corralling bulls, you know. Y'all should have plenty of extra time, seeing how I won't need a ride to Houston this week."

Once again, Monte wondered if his aunt was trying to find reasons for him and Evie to spend more time together. He suppressed a sigh. Despite the nonexistent state of his love life, he didn't need a matchmaker. Nor did he have any intention of building anything more than a professional relationship with their temporary caregiver.

"Speaking of treatments." He forked a chunk of syrupy pancakes. "Last night, a friend forwarded me information on clinical trials for ovarian cancer. I haven't read through the material yet but will prioritize doing so today."

His aunt frowned and looked at her plate.

Did she think he'd lost faith in her current treatment plan? He shouldn't have said anything until he'd learned more.

Although he shifted the conversation to something more pleasant, the spark he'd seen in her eyes first thing this morning seemed faded.

He sensed she could use a dash of humor this afternoon.

Accompanying Evie as she walked the girls out of the house, he encouraged the twins to give one of their impromptu plays once they returned from school.

"Can you and Ms. Evie be in the show, too?" Luna asked.

Callie jumped up and down. "Yeah! With the stage and curtains, remember?"

He did recall her request that he build her something like that, but not how he had responded. "That'll take time, Cowpoke. I was hoping y'all could pull something together today."

"But that won't be real."

Apparently, her visit to Ms. Vargas's classroom had elevated her expectations.

"You promised," she whined.

While he doubted that, considering he'd forgotten his reply, he felt it best to concede in case she was right. He couldn't teach them to stand by their word if he wasn't willing to do the same.

"Okay. I'll start working on that this afternoon."

Callie skipped ahead, then turned back around to make eye contact with Evie. "Will you make the curtains?"

"I don't have anything to make them with."

"Aunt Martha has a sewing machine and bunches and bunches of fabric in the attic."

"I don't know how to sew."

The girls stared at her with wide eyes, as if this was the strangest thing they'd heard since she told them she'd never attended a rodeo.

Luna slipped her hand into Evie's. "That's okay. They have YouTube videos."

Evie burst out laughing, and the sound was so contagious, soon they all joined her.

"Okay." She gave a quick nod. "I'll see what I can do."

"Yay!" Both girls cheered and started jumping up and down.

Her expression sobered. "Don't get too excited yet. When it comes to anything creative, I'm all thumbs. But I'll do my best."

His heart swelled at the lighthearted interaction the four of them shared. This was precisely the type of moments he'd dreamed of enjoying with his wife. He'd been devastated when she left, and he had decided he was done with women for good. Too bad Evie didn't plan to stick around. She was the type of gal that could make a man rethink how he planned to spend the rest of his life.

* * *

Once back at the house, Monte excused himself to exercise his bulls and Evie spent the morning cleaning and tending to his aunt. After the doctor's recommendation from the day before, Evie would've expected her to feel discouraged. Yet, she seemed chipper, even energized.

Had the smoothies Evie made for her helped that much? If so, she needed to make sure the Bowmans kept plenty of fruit and protein shakes on hand.

Laundry taken care of, she followed the sound of humming into the living room to find Martha sitting in an armchair, knitting.

This reminded her of the girls' request from that morning.

Martha glanced up as she approached. Smiling, she looked around. "Everything appears all clean and tidy. Might be an opportunity to take some time to yourself. Have you been to the lake, yet? There's a lovely walking path."

"Actually, I was wondering if I could borrow your sewing machine."

"Of course, dear. It's in the attic. The door on the wall across from your bed leads to our storage area. Don't worry, it's not as small and dark as one might expect. But if you're more comfortable, I can ask Monte to retrieve it for you."

"That's not necessary, but thank you."

"We have a lovely fabric store in town. Although I have a lot of unused supplies tucked away in tubs that you're welcome to."

"I appreciate that."

Once in the attic, she was grateful to find it more spacious, and with a flick of a switch, brighter, than she'd anticipated.

An antique chest like the ones people once used as suitcases when they traveled and various other items from a similar time period occupied the corner nearest a small window. Along two walls, numerous tubs stood one on top of the other, and sagging boxes lined the third.

She picked up a Raggedy Ann doll with yellowing fabric, a threadbare foot and a fraying apron. Had this once belonged to Martha? Books, some with thick, maroon or green hard covers, others leatherback, were stacked in front of a pedestal table with a scallop-edged surface and intricately carved legs.

She crossed the room to where a handful of quilts, some pastel, others in vibrant designs, hung from a rack. Behind this stood a series of tubs, some labeled Fabric, others Buttons and Threads, and still others, Patterns. Intrigued, she knelt and opened the latter. Amused by the styles, she imagined for whom Martha might have created the clothing.

Where might they have placed her sewing machine? As she glanced about, she noticed a picture frame lying on the ground beneath an old chair. She picked it up. Although faded by time, the photograph was of a slightly younger Monte, on his wedding day. He was leaning in to kiss a woman with long blond hair, wearing an elegant white gown with intricate beading and lace flowers.

That had to be his ex.

The two looked so happy. What had happened between them?

Did he still love her?

It wasn't her business.

She returned the frame and continued her search for Martha's sewing machine. Ten minutes later, she'd found it and also some forest green velvety fabric that would make great stage curtains. With the cloth draped over her shoulder, she started to carry the machine down the retractable stairs but then thought better of it.

She wouldn't be able to run after Callie, were she to stumble and twist her ankle, nor did she want to accidentally drop and break Martha's machine. She'd ask Monte to bring it down for her when he came home.

In the hall, she paused, a jolt shooting through her at the

sound of his voice. Resisting the smile tugging on her mouth, she forced confidence into her steps and strode down the hall toward the kitchen.

"I know it's been a difficult journey."

The concern in his tone halted her before she rounded the corner.

"I'm missing so many precious moments with the girls." Martha sounded deflated.

"They understand. And once you beat this thing, you and the twins will have plenty of time together. Just keep fighting for a little longer."

"I don't have any fight left."

"You're just tired."

"It's more than that. I don't want to spend however few days—"

"Years. Decades, probably."

"You remember what the oncologist said. Even if—"

"He was just being cautious. You know how doctors are. They've got to tell you about the worst-case scenario. But he doesn't know you like I do. You can do this."

"I don't want to waste the rest of my life lying around in bed. I want to enjoy the girls while I still can."

Evie turned the corner to see Monte kiss his aunt's cheek.

"You're probably hungry."

He glanced up as Evie entered, and setting the fabric on a nearby counter, she asked for help lugging the machine down, after she'd just assured Martha she could manage that herself.

"No problem." He dashed out and returned with the machine as if it were as light as a box of cereal. He placed it in the center of the table. "Think you could make my aunt a shake—with protein added?"

She donned her widest, most encouraging smile. "I would love to. Would you like one as well?"

He looked at the time on the microwave. "You know what? Why not? I could use a break."

They occupied the next hour or so sharing stories—mostly about when Monte was a little boy. He'd spent a good deal of his summers at his aunt's and, apparently, had been as energetic as Callie. He'd also fantasized about becoming an entomologist when he grew up. Then, of becoming a pilot, then an astronaut, and finally, a country-Western singer.

Laughing, he shook his head. "That last one is hilarious, considering how much I hate standing in front of crowds. Meaning, groups with more than five people." He looked at his aunt. "You should have given me a reality check."

"I had no intention of teaching you not to pursue your dreams. I knew the good Lord, your passions and life experiences would lead you where you needed to go. Not that I ever thought that would be to a ranch in Texas."

He turned to Evie. "I grew up in the Golden State."

Her eyebrows shot up. "Really?" He didn't seem the Californian type.

"Son of a teacher and an accountant."

"How'd you get into the rodeo world?"

"Had a friend who lived out of town. His parents raised horses and were deep into local cowboy culture. Didn't take me long to catch the bug." He snatched a cookie from a plateful Martha had placed in the center of the table. "But I didn't ride bulls until I came to Texas for college. Started on a dare."

His aunt rolled her eyes. "It's only by God's grace y'all are still breathing, with how you boys used to challenge one another." She looked at Evie. "Thankfully, he always told me after the fact." She leveled a gaze on her nephew. "I suspect you only shared a fraction of your escapades."

He chuckled. "Didn't want to give you too much cause to worry."

This led to all the ways Callie was similar, which his aunt

joked was God's way of getting him back for all the lack of sleep he'd caused her.

Monte gulped down the last of his smoothie and stood. "Guess I best get back to it." He faced Evie. "Walk me out?"

Her pulse increased a notch, and she fought a silly smile threatening to break through. She nodded and followed him to the porch.

He released a sigh. "Seems my aunt could use more encouragement than I realized." Rubbing the back of his neck, he gazed into the distance, then brightened. "I've got an idea. I'll build us a bonfire tonight. Got me a sizeable burn pile I need to take care of anyway. I'll bring my guitar and we can sing silly songs, roast marshmallows and make s'mores."

"You play?"

"Just for fun."

Could this man be any more charming?

He must've taken her delay as disinterest, because he added, "If you don't want to come—"

"No, that sounds fun." She'd spoken with too much enthusiasm. Heat seeped into her face. "I love spending time with your girls."

And you.

She shouldn't be thinking that way. Why was it so difficult to remember that she was here for a brief period of time—perhaps even shorter, if his aunt decided to stop treatment.

If that occurred, Evie could be gone by week's end.

Chapter Eight

Monte was checking his cattle for illness and injury when he saw Evie drive by, heading to pick up the girls.

Was it that time already? The day sure seemed to be galloping by, and he hadn't even made it through half his herd. His periodic trips to the house, including nearly an hour for lunch, hadn't helped his chore list any.

But he'd been concerned for his aunt.

While that was true, it didn't explain why he found himself looking for Evie the moment he stepped inside. Nor why he had to fight an almost goofy grin whenever she engaged him in conversation, regardless of the subject.

Had he ever reacted this way with the twins' mom? In the beginning, maybe. Toward the end, their interactions had more frequently brought sorrow than joy as he slowly came to realize his love wasn't enough to hold her.

Would she have stayed, had he been willing to give up his PBR dreams?

Would he have?

She'd never given him the chance, which proved she'd set her heart on leaving. She'd never been the country-loving type.

That was a trait Evie shared, it seemed, which was the very reason he remained focused on his bulls despite a ridiculous urge to chase after her now.

He'd just finished inspecting the leg of a limping derby,

unfortunately one of his more athletic, when his daughter called out to him.

Wiping dust from his hands, he jogged across the pasture and through the gate to wait for them. Luna raced toward him and reached him out of breath, face red. Callie followed at a pace much slower than usual.

"Well, now, look who blew in with the tumbleweeds." Grabbing them beneath their arms, he lifted the girls one after the other, swung them in the air, then dropped them, laughing, to their feet. "You have fun at school?"

Luna nodded and told him about all the art supplies she'd used and books she'd read.

By now Evie, who'd followed at a more casual pace, had joined them, her eyes gleaming with amusement. Honey-toned streaks in her strawberry blond hair shimmered in the sun.

"That sounds like quite a day." He turned to Callie. "What about you? Was it as boring as you'd thought?"

She shrugged and squatted down, picked up a stick and began to draw in the dirt.

Not the enthusiasm he'd hoped for, but at least she didn't say she hated it. "Make any friends?"

"Sort of."

Either the child was plumb tuckered out or she was in a funk about something. Had someone teased or excluded her? "Did you play with anyone at recess?"

Her eyes brightened as she launched into a story about challenging her classmates to races and rolling down the sloping hill behind the school.

He quirked an eyebrow at her. "That explains the grass streaks on your outfit."

She glanced at her jeans. "Sorry."

He couldn't say her appearance surprised him. That child could soil an outfit faster than she could walk out the door.

Almost made him wonder why he didn't just let her wear her playclothes.

But Aunt Martha would never let Callie leave the house looking like a prairie dog digging through the turnip patch, as she liked to say.

"Dirt, fabric and little girls wash up well enough." He bopped her on the nose.

She scrunched her face, probably thinking of her upcoming bath.

That was his Callie.

After some prodding, whatever mood she'd arrived home with lifted, and she began jabbering on about what the other students brought for lunch.

"*Everyone* gets juice boxes?" he asked.

"Unless they buy chocolate milk. Only Pete said it smelled bad, so nobody wanted any." She was halfway through a story about a boy who stole someone else's dessert when Max caught her attention.

She darted off toward him.

Reaching the porch, Monte shook his head. "To think, in ten years or so, I'll hardly get a word out of her, if what folks with teenagers say is true."

Evie laughed. "I can't imagine that child holding her tongue at any age."

"Good point." Taking Luna by the hand, he led the way up the steps and into the house, pleased to see his aunt in the living room working on one of her scrapbooks. Lucy had encouraged her to do things that brought her joy as a way of increasing her resiliency.

That reminded him… "Y'all up for a good ol' weenie roast for supper?" He relayed his bonfire idea.

"It won't be too cold?" Aunt Martha asked.

"Not with jackets. Weather app said high fifties."

His aunt's face lit up. "That sounds lovely. Let me check on our chocolate bar stash."

Hand cupped over his mouth, he leaned toward Evie, and her soft floral scent momentarily halted his thoughts. "She's got a secret hiding place, so the girls can't get to it."

"Smart. If you're out, I can run to the store."

"Sounds good."

He really had no logical reason to stick around, not with the amount of ranch work he still needed to tackle. His reluctance to leave didn't make much more sense, either.

Nor would he waste time considering the emotions emerging behind it.

"Guess I best get." He gave Luna a sideways hug, hollered an *I love you* to his aunt, and spent the next couple hours trying to focus on his herd. But his thoughts kept pinging between Evie, who always made him smile, and his aunt, which knotted his stomach.

He understood how tough everything had been for her, physically. He knew well how devastating it must've felt when she first learned her cancer had returned. That news had nearly wrecked them all. He also realized how, considering the what-ifs conveyed with her diagnosis, she might feel as if too much was stacked against her.

But she couldn't quit treatment.

Father, give her strength. Please.

The girls had already lost their mother. They couldn't lose their beloved aunt as well.

He wouldn't let that happen.

Eyeing a truck that belonged to one of his ranch hands, parked a few feet from his, he scanned his property for sight of the guy. Hopefully he was repairing that rotten pole barn post. Travis was handy that way. Tended to be intuitive with the bulls, too. Had a gut instinct as to which were the winners and which they needed to send to auction.

With the man's help, with Monte's growing experience and what was looking to be a genetically solid herd, his animal athletes stood a shot at bringing in sizable earnings. Then, maybe he could hire a full-time nanny.

Evie's smiling face popped into his mind. With a mental shake, he returned to the pasture and the bull he'd been inspecting prior. Noting swelling, he abandoned his hopes that the issue would resolve itself and called the vet.

He explained what he'd found and when he first noticed it. "Thought maybe he needed a shot of Lutalyse."

"He competing this weekend?"

"No, thank goodness." Although he had hoped to enter the bull into the Christmas charity event he planned to take Evie and the girls to.

"Okay. Because I might not be able to come out until early next week. Unless I can squeeze in a stop by your place on my way to the Johnson ranch."

"That sounds great."

"Need me to call before I come?"

"Nah. If I'm not around, one of my ranch hands will be." The less fuss he caused, the more likely the doc would find room in his already busy schedule.

He'd barely hung up when his phone chimed a text. Seeing it was Evie, he grinned, then chuckled when he read her question. Seemed the girls were trying to hornswoggle her into believing they always had ice cream with their s'mores, and Evie wanted to know if he thought it too cold for that.

He replied with a series of laughing emojis that soon led to a hilarious GIF exchange.

One that had him looking forward to the evening much more than he should've been—and every night after.

Until it came time for her to leave.

Evie placed graham crackers, chocolate bars, marshmallows and thermoses of hot cocoa into one of Martha's totes.

She'd moved to the fridge to gather condiments for hot dogs when her phone rang.

She glanced at the number on her screen, smiled and answered. "Savannah! How are you? Still causing mischief in Memphis?"

"You know me. Always got to play big." Savannah laughed and shared a few of her most recent escapades, most of which involved food. "How's life in the country? Met any handsome cowboys yet?"

An image of Monte's easy grin and hazel eyes came to mind, sending a rush of heat to her face. She shook it off with a nervous chuckle and shifted the conversation to a much safer topic—the children. "Callie is as wild-spirited as she is adorable. One of these days, she's liable to find her way into one of the pastures and try to climb onto a bull's back."

"Sounds like you've got quite an assignment. Guess you're glad it'll be over soon."

Her heart sank at the thought, but then she reminded herself of her long-term goals. "I'm just hoping next time, they'll place me somewhere close to a reputable nursing college."

"Actually, that's why I'm calling. Mr. McGee asked me if I'm interested in going to Philadelphia for an extended gig. While he wouldn't promise anything, he said to plan on at least nine months, and likely longer. Isn't that one of the cities you put on your preference list?"

She felt a burst of excitement tempered by a twinge of sadness knowing her time in Sage Creek would soon come to an end. Yet, why hadn't their boss called her? "Yeah. When is the start date?"

"Ten days from now."

"That's quick. And so close to Christmas."

"I don't know the full story, but the grandson caring for the woman suddenly decided it's more than he can manage on his own."

"Alzheimer's?"

"Dementia. It's a part-time deal but with full room and board, obviously. Figured it'd be perfect for you, with you wanting to go to school and all."

"Only problem is my replacement isn't due for another couple of weeks." That was probably why their boss hadn't reached out to her.

"Think you can finagle an earlier end date? Maybe talk the family you're with into cutting you loose early? That wouldn't leave them on their own for long. Didn't they manage well enough between when they sent Tracy packing and you arrived?"

Monte probably would let her leave early if she told him why. "I doubt Mr. McGee would be open to that."

"Oh, I don't know. You *have* bailed him out a few times when others dropped the ball. Your current placement is proof of that. Seems to me, he may be willing to accommodate you just to keep you happy. So you'll stick around. You *are* one of his better, and longest-lasting, caregivers."

There tended to be a high turnover rate in this field, mainly because people eventually tired of all the travel. She also knew Mr. McGee wanted her to earn her nursing degree almost as much as she did. That was, if she remained with New Day. Contractually, she'd have to, if she accepted the company's tuition reimbursement.

This conversation was causing a hollowed feeling in her gut. From guilt, or was she disappointed at the prospect of leaving the ranch earlier than anticipated?

If so, that was one reason she felt tempted to follow Savannah's suggestion. The longer she stayed, the harder it would be to leave when the time came. But she wasn't willing to do anything that might add to Monte and his family's stress. Integrity demanded she honor her commitment.

She'd simply have to trust that God would present her with

something even better than the Philadelphia placement—in His perfect timing. She'd log into the company database this week to review other upcoming opportunities. Hopefully, another city with a great nursing college would be listed soon.

But it still stung to think her being here had prevented her from what sounded like a perfect assignment.

Callie burst in and began rummaging through the cupboard where the Bowmans kept their food storage containers. Leaving a handful of bowls and tubs scattered on the floor, she darted into the pantry. All her clattering suggested she was making another mess.

Evie didn't know whether to feel frustrated or amused. "I've got to go before one of the munchkins breaks something. Or hurts herself."

She ended the call and went to Callie, who stood on the chair, on tiptoes, reaching for a galvanized bucket. "Need help?"

The child nodded. "Can you get that down for me?" She pointed. "I want to make an ocean habitat."

Evie immediately thought of the mud experience. At least Callie was wearing her playclothes. "I love your creativity." She surveyed the items already pulled from the shelves, imagining the living room in a similar state. "How about you choose one container and put the rest away. Then, if you give me a minute to check on your aunt—"

"She's talking to Ms. Lucy on the phone."

Evie nodded. "Then, we can design something together."

Callie frowned and angled her head as if not entirely pleased with the suggestion—most likely because of the tidying up it involved. But the activity won out. With Luna joining, the three of them traipsed outside to gather twigs, brush and whatever other nature items the girls found useful.

This soon led to the twins searching under rocks for bugs.

By the time Monte returned home and everyone headed

out for the bonfire, the sun was sinking beneath the distant tree line and painting the sky in vibrant pinks and purples.

Wearing jackets, the girls rode ahead on Side-by-Side with Aunt Martha, who sported a scarf around her neck. This led Evie and Monte to stroll through the grasslands alone, an action their beautiful surroundings made much too intimate. Carrying a tote filled with s'mores supplies, she eyed the guitar hanging from a strap over his shoulder.

She was anxious to hear him sing. Not that she needed reasons to find him more endearing.

Averting her thoughts, she plucked up a long blade of straw and began snapping it into smaller pieces. "It sure is peaceful out here." She inhaled the clean-smelling air. "It's almost like God feels closer, know what I mean?"

He smiled. "I do. That's one of the things I love most about ranching. It's a lot easier to hear from God when there isn't a lot of noise competing for my attention. Makes life a lot… clearer, and whatever steps He leads me to take, firmer."

"I admire your desire to follow Christ."

"Figure that's a necessity in my business. It comes with a lot of uncertainty and unknowns. A man can do everything right, working hard from sunup to sundown, and still land himself in debt. But with one talented bull, he can become wildly successful as well."

"Sort of like coaching humans, huh?"

He laughed. "That's exactly what it's like. Always hoping for the Olympic champion, running the drills, building the endurance. Praying for the day when talent, drive and preparation merge into the next superstar. The hard truth is, I can't afford to invest in every calf. Each year, I have to cull my herd, trusting God will help me know which ones to auction and which to train."

She raised her eyebrows. "Train?"

He nodded. "They need to learn when to turn it on, when to chill. How to behave themselves in the bucking chutes."

"Interesting. What makes for a great bull?"

"They're scored on spin, how high they kick, that sort of thing. But the champions are intuitive. They sense when the cowboy's weight shifts, and react accordingly."

They reached the top of his property, where Monte had built a sizable mound of branches and twigs. Aunt Martha and Luna were sitting side by side, each on one of the stumps positioned as chairs while her sister climbed a nearby tree.

Upon seeing her dad, Callie raced over. "Can I help light the fire?"

"Yep." He led the way to the wood debris, and soon, orange and red flames danced against the darkening horizon.

Sitting with Callie to her left, Monte to her right, Evie took a slow, deep breath. "The smell of smoke reminds me of my church camp days, back when I was a little girl."

He pierced a marshmallow with his roasting stick. "Happy memories?"

She chuckled. "Mostly, minus a belly ache or two."

Initially, he led them in silly songs about bellowing bullfrogs and slippery soap, adapting the lyrics to whatever phrase one of the girls tossed out.

Laughing, Evie joined in. "Then along came a salamander, slithering up the tree then down, before falling to the ground." She could get used to evenings like this.

"Bam!" Callie sprang to her feet and clapped her hands.

Everyone laughed.

Evie had done a lot of that lately. It felt good to be silly. She couldn't remember the last time she'd allowed her playful side to emerge.

Maybe she needed to view the Philadelphia gig and her time in Sage Creek differently. Less like a letdown and more like something of a God-given vacation.

Minus chasing after a wiggly, squiggly, easily bored little girl, not that she minded. In fact, she'd enjoyed every moment much more than she'd expected. Plus, she wasn't having any trouble getting her steps in. That was an unexpected bonus she couldn't say when caring strictly for the elderly.

"Daddy?" Luna's face glowed in the light of the campfire. "Can you sing the song you wrote for my birthday?"

Monte smiled and slowed the tempo. A tranquil hush fell over the space as he began to sing about his love for his daughter. He spoke of the moment he first held her, of the overwhelming emotions that had invaded his heart. He relayed the day she released her grip on his finger to stumble forward into her first steps. Of hearing her first words and watching her appreciation for beauty draw her to the wildflowers sprouting along the fence line.

Looking from one twin to the next, he broadened the verse to include them both:

"I'll always fight for you. See the best in you.

And when your legs feel ready to give way,

By your side I'll always stay,

I'll take you by the hand,

Lend my strength till you can stand,

Until the bright rays of dawn break through."

Tears stung Evie's eyes, feeling, through his words, the depth of love he felt for the twins.

What would it feel like to have someone sing like that to her?

Maybe someday, she'd find out. Although her gut told her there weren't many men like Monte in the world.

Chapter Nine

Saturday morning, after tending to the animals, Monte invited the girls to help build their stage. They urged Evie to join them, evidence of how quickly they'd become attached to her.

He could understand why. She was kind, gentle, attentive and witty. And unlike his ex-wife, she wasn't afraid to act silly. He recalled the night before, her melodious laughter, and the soft glow of the campfire's light on her face.

For a moment, he'd fantasized about sending the girls and Aunt Martha back to the house, so that he could have Evie to himself. Then, of holding her hand as they walked back together under the starry night sky.

He needed to stop thinking that way.

"You girls want to help me drive in some nails?" He handed them each a hammer, set a large sheet of plywood on top of two pallets he'd placed side by side, then motioned them over. He gave them a nail then marked Xs where they'd drive them, with enough room apart so that they wouldn't accidentally whack one another. "Watch your fingers, now."

Taking her father's advice to heart, Luna gently tapped while Callie, ever the risk-taker, used enough force to make him wince. "Careful, Cowpoke. You'll need all ten digits for mutton busting."

"This weekend?"

He shook his head. "Next."

She groaned. "That's a long way away."

He chuckled. "Forever. I know."

"Can we practice?"

He and Evie exchanged an amused look, her smile making him feel like they'd just shared a moment. "How do you figure, seeing how we don't have any sheep?"

"Sebastian does. He's in my class, and we're best friends."

"Are you now?"

She nodded. "We both like playing with our dogs and catching crawfish and eating strawberry ice cream. And running fast at recess."

He smiled, picturing the two of them racing up and down the hill behind the school building.

"Well, now." Evie raised a brow. "That sounds like a match made in heaven."

Callie nodded. "He wants me to come to his house to play, only he's not sure his mom will let me. She gets grumpy when he acts too rowdy or doesn't listen like he should."

"I hear that," Monte teased.

His daughter used her forearm to swipe her hair out of her face. "He's probably afraid we'll have too much fun and he'll forget the rules."

Evie laughed. "An understandable concern."

His daughter set down her hammer and looked at Monte. "Can you come? Then you could watch us and his mom wouldn't have to worry."

Invite himself to someone else's home? That sounded all kinds of awkward. "I'll think about it."

"Can we go after supper?"

"Nope. Got someone coming to learn bull riding."

"Ms. Evie can take me."

He shook his head. "It's her off night, remember?"

"No fair. I wish I had a mama. Then I could go see friends whenever I wanted."

A lump lodged in his throat at the thread of truth to her

words. While having a mother wouldn't give her the limitless social life she claimed, he figured her lack had probably cost her more than a few playdates. He'd heard the ladies at church making plans with one another often enough to know that. He doubted any of them excluded his girls intentionally. They were simply friends who met on occasion and brought their kids along.

Was Callie merely frustrated that he hadn't responded to her request as she'd hoped? Or did she know about those get-togethers and feel left out?

If so, what could he say to help her understand without hurting her further?

His aunt would probably tell him it was time he started dating. When was he supposed to do that? He was having a tough enough time managing everything as it was. Besides, he didn't want to subject the girls to more loss. What if he became involved with someone, his daughters grew attached, and then the lady bailed?

They'd already had one woman walk out on them.

No one spoke for a while after that, the steady clanging of metal against metal almost loud in the absence of conversation.

"Mind if I play some music?" Evie raised her phone.

"Not at all."

He was intrigued when she played something from the seventies.

He paused to listen. "Reminds me of the summer I worked at an ice cream store. The owner had a track of maybe ten songs he cycled through. That era was one of them. Played so often, lyrics rolled through my head at the oddest times."

She laughed. "Hope I'm not bringing back traumatic memories."

"Nah. Those were fun times."

"This music reminds me of summer road trips with my grandmother."

"Y'all go anywhere exciting?"

"She thought so, although my ten-, eleven- and twelve-year-old self didn't appreciate quilt museums, historical homes and factory tours as much as she did. Yet, just being with her made everything fun. Special. The long car rides included. Probably because I had a captive audience." She threw him a playful grin.

"You were a big talker, I take it?"

"Oh, my, yes. She called me her little storyteller. Said I could spin a tale better than Shakespeare himself. Except mine were true. Mostly."

"No wonder you and my Callie get along so well." He winked at his daughter, who'd looked up upon the mention of her name. "You and your grandmother close?"

"We were. She passed a few summers ago. Heart attack."

"Sorry to hear that." She probably understood, in a way Tracy Gray had never seemed to, all the emotions he and his girls felt related to his aunt's diagnosis. He hated knowing Evie could relate to their pain but was grateful to think this would intensify her desire to fight for his aunt's life.

Her being here now, helping build this stage—and agreeing to the children's performance plans—was evidence of that.

To think he'd been so frustrated when she first arrived. Now he was beginning to wonder if God had sent her here as a gift.

Too bad she wasn't staying.

But would she—could she—if asked? Seemed that might be the most efficient option for everyone. Why go through the trouble of sending someone to replace her, unless she was already scheduled somewhere else.

She most likely was. He sighed and checked the time on his phone. Brushing dust from his hands, he straightened. "Best corral my bulls into the sorting alleys so I'm ready for the kid coming to ride."

Callie sprang to her feet. "Can we come?"

"Don't see why not."

"Yay!"

Luna appeared equally excited, although, unlike her sister, her feet remained planted on the ground. She turned to Evie. "Are you coming, too?"

Assuming she'd rather spend the rest of the day relaxing, he started to give her an out.

She responded before he could.

"That sounds interesting." Her bright-eyed grin indicated she wasn't just trying to be polite.

Maybe country life was growing on her.

He rested a hand on his belt buckle. "You sure?"

She nodded. "I'd love to see more of what you do."

She may as well have said she was interested in *him*, with how her statement accelerated his pulse—a reaction he immediately chastised himself for. Why did his heart and head keep toying with thoughts of something that would never be?

Smiling, Luna slipped her hand into Evie's while Callie darted ahead. After a few paces, she turned back around. "Are you going to run them, too?"

He gazed at the nearby pasture. "May not be a bad idea to tucker them out some."

Evie's eyes widened, probably envisioning him chasing after the massive creatures on foot.

He stifled a laugh. "On ATVs."

Her taut expression indicated she didn't find that prospect any less concerning. But she didn't say anything or make a dash for the house.

After he'd circled the pasture a few times, the girls giggling and whooping him on, the bulls darting this way and that, Evie's posture had relaxed considerably.

He'd even caught an amused glint in her eye a time or two.

He had just parked near the arena when his phone chimed a text from Ian.

Monte looked at Evie. "Y'all want to go for a spin? The guy I'll be working with tonight's going to be late." And hadn't bothered to let him know until five minutes before he was due to arrive. Then again, his uncle had indicated the young man wasn't the most responsible in town.

Her eyes widened, and her hand flew to her neck. "Oh, no. I couldn't possibly."

"I do! I do!" The twins jumped up and down, chanting in unison.

"Come on, then." He motioned for them to follow him.

"Wait." Evie darted after them. "How about we go inside for some cookies. And I'll help you build a fort, or we could play that bouncing hippo game you both like so much." Her words tumbled out so fast, she seemed to run out of breath.

Actually, she looked near terrified.

Did she think he meant on a bull?

He stifled a chuckle. "I meant on ATVs."

Her cheeks turned the most endearing shade of pink. "Oh. Right." She offered a shy smile. "That sounds fun. If you've got time."

"Yep. Got our two-seaters in the equipment shed."

As expected, Callie had made it halfway there before the rest of them reached the chicken coop.

Luna slipped her hand into Evie's once again, an action Monte was apt to feel jealous of, if he didn't keep his head on straight.

"Ms. Evie," his daughter said, "can I ride with you?"

A lump lodged in his throat at the tender, almost maternal way Evie looked down at his child. "I would love that."

If only he could meet someone like her in Sage Creek, he'd be more inclined to follow his aunt's dating advice.

But something told him finding a woman like Evie was about as rare as raising a PBR superstar.

* * *

With Evie on the ATV, the engine rumbling beneath her and vibrating her handlebars, Luna climbed on behind her and grabbed on to either side of her seat.

Beside them, Monte and Callie idled on a similar vehicle, a 2UP, he called it. "Ready to kick up dirt?"

A burst of excitement erupted into a wide grin. She glanced back to find her little friend smiling just as wide, eyes bright. "What do you say? Think we can take them?"

Her thin brow furrowed. "Where?"

Monte laughed. "She means race us, peanut. And to that, we'd say…" With a mischievous twist of his mouth, he revved his engine and the two of them took off.

"Hey, no fair!" Turning the throttle, she followed as fast as her newbie nerves allowed.

Initially, she tensed with every jostling pothole, slowing when rounding the corner. By the time they reached the far pasture, blessedly free of bulls, she gained confidence to accelerate to twenty-five miles per hour.

She loved the feel of the crisp wind on her face and blowing through her hair and the scent of the earth swirling up around her.

Dropping back to meet her, Monte gave her a thumbs-up sign. "There you go!"

Behind him, Callie extended her legs and chanted, "Faster! Faster!"

Monte continued to match Evie's speed. It felt like they were experiencing this moment together, as if he was enjoying spending time with her.

She'd once read that shared adventures formed and strengthened bonds. Was that why she felt increasingly drawn to him now?

Did he feel the same connection to her that she was feeling, at this moment, to him and the girls?

That was ridiculous, of course. If anything, he was delighting in his children and some good, clean fun, and nothing more.

She needed to view this little jaunt in the same way.

Yet, her experience with Monte *was* revealing something she'd sensed increasingly during the past year—she was tired of living single. She longed for someone with whom she could share laughter, frustrations, tears and dreams. And God willing, children to fill their home with giggles, silly songs and ATV rides in the country.

But there was a problem. Rural settings didn't tend to have nursing colleges, and she couldn't give up her goal to earn a degree, even if he were to ask—and she highly doubted he ever would.

If she detoured from her plans and things didn't work out between her and Monte, or any man, for that matter, she could easily land in a hot mess, financially speaking.

Nearing the tree line, Monte slowed. "Probably should head back now. See if my bull-riding student actually showed."

She nodded. "I better check on Aunt Martha. And get supper started." She was thinking of trying a new recipe she'd found online.

Monte chuckled when Luna's groan matched her sister's. "Another time."

The thought sent a jolt through Evie, and she fought against an overly enthusiastic smile.

Focusing on the pasture ahead instead of her growing feelings for Monte, which she had no intention of exploring or feeding further, she accompanied him back to the arena. As he'd predicted, a tall, broad-shouldered guy who didn't look much older than eighteen, was waiting for him.

He wore dingy blue jeans that seemed to hang from his frame, boots and a sweatshirt that sagged sideways. Chin-length black hair extended at least three inches beneath his sweat-stained ballcap.

Monte introduced him as Ian, a friend's nephew. "This here's Evie Bell. Drove down from Dallas."

She gave a nod. "But I'm originally from Grand Rapids, Michigan."

The guy widened his stance. "River City, huh? What brought you to Sage Creek?"

Monte answered for her. "She's taking care of my aunt for a spell."

"Speaking of, I should probably check on her now."

Feet on the bottom rail of the arena gate and hands gripping the top, Callie hung backwards. "Can we stay with you, Daddy?"

"So long as you're not underfoot and don't go running off without asking."

Luna looked from her dad to Evie, as if torn between the two. But then, probably looking forward to some extra time with her father, chose to remain. The fact that Evie factored into her decision at all touched her.

She returned to the house to find Aunt Martha in the kitchen, singing along to Southern gospel playing from an old-fashioned, portable radio. She wore a red-and-green checked apron and her hair was pulled back beneath a silky green bandanna. Flour, sugar, a mixing bowl and other items cluttered the counter to the right of the sink. To her left, she'd set out vegetables, a cutting board and a chunk of some type of meat wrapped in butcher paper.

She glanced over as Evie entered. "Hello, dear. Y'all sure seemed to be having fun out there this afternoon." She motioned with her spatula to the window. "The girls will build up an appetite tonight. I'm making their favorite. Beef potpie. And pound cake drizzled with cherry pie filling for dessert."

"Sounds delicious." Evie went to wash her hands. "I've

not made any of those before, but I'm a quick learner. Just tell me what to do."

When the oven beeped, Martha placed a cake pan filled with creamy yellow batter inside and set the timer.

"I've got this." She waved a hand. "You go enjoy more of that lovely evening air. I'm rather enjoying myself. It does a heart good to make food for one's family, don't you think?"

Evie couldn't say, as she hadn't had that experience yet, unless one counted the times her parents had forced her to cook during her teenage years. Back then, she would've much preferred to spend time with her friends.

But she could see how much pleasure Martha was experiencing doing something that she might not have felt well enough to do previously.

While Evie knew that if pushed, the woman would allow her to participate, she also sensed Martha preferred to be left alone to create. And, based on the way she'd been singing a moment ago, to connect with God.

"Okay," Evie said. "If you're sure."

"I am."

She watched her for a moment longer, happy to see Martha's increased energy and enthusiasm. This was quite a change from the day she'd fallen. Was this due to the smoothies she'd been drinking or the break in her treatment?

Maybe both.

Hopefully, it would last. The woman deserved every drop of joy and vigor possible.

Of course, it hadn't slipped Evie's notice that Martha also seemed particularly pleased whenever she and Monte spent time together.

Apparently, both her and Martha's hearts were struggling to remember how fast Evie's departure date was approaching.

Discarding the thought, she stepped onto the porch and gazed toward the arena. A few bulls waited, seemingly calm, in the alley, as Monte called it, while he stood in a nearby grassy patch next to Ian. It looked like Monte was showing his student, who sat on a big stability ball, body positioning and drills.

Appreciating the pleasant temperatures, which were considerably warmer than Michigan's winters, she decided to use her unexpected free time to catch up on some reading. Her mom had recommended a book from a new author and would probably want to talk about it when they next spoke. Evie loved those discussions as much as her mom.

Sitting in the rocking chair near the end of the porch, she rested her feet on the edge of a flowerpot and opened her phone's e-reader. A few chapters in, something the heroine said reminded her of her conversation with her coworker.

She decided to check the company database.

Only about half a dozen open assignments were listed. Unfortunately, two started before her current placement ended. One was for a small town in Arkansas she'd never heard of, and another wouldn't begin for six weeks. The final listing wasn't in a bad location, but it would only last for one month. Still, it might be a good backup, because while she'd love to hold out for a Philadelphia-type assignment, she did have bills to pay.

Calling her boss, she stood and rested her elbows on the porch railing, her eyes on the horse stables and surrounding pastures.

Expecting his voice mail, she was surprised when he picked up. "Evie, hello. How are things in the Lone Star State?"

"Fine, thank you." She broached the subject of future assignments.

"Things are a tad slower than we'd expected. Has rural living grown on you any?"

Monte has.

The thought jolted her and was entirely unwelcome. "It has its pluses."

"Enough that you might give the opening in Arkansas a harder look? I know you're aiming for the city, and we'll get you there. May not be this year, but I promise you this—we won't forget your preferred list, or how you filled in for the Bowmans."

"That's what frustrates me. Knowing my coming here cost me such a great location, in terms of my long-term career goals. And as far as Arkansas goes, you know I prefer to avoid small towns." Although she had to admit, this ranch had grown on her. "Current placement aside," she amended.

"I get it, and I'll do everything in my power to see you in an area with a fabulous nursing school."

"I appreciate that." Rubbing her temple, she ended the call.

Determining not to let what felt like an unfair setback dampen an otherwise lovely day, she released a breath and turned around to find Monte standing near the steps.

Based on his tense expression, he'd caught at least part of her conversation and wasn't pleased. Why would he be? She might as well have said that she regretted coming here.

Her stomach felt queasy, almost like she'd betrayed a friend.

He looked at her a moment longer, then turned and left without a word.

Oh, well. Maybe his overhearing her wasn't entirely a bad thing—if it provided the emotional distance she was struggling to maintain.

Chapter Ten

Sunday morning, Monte returned from feeding the animals to find Evie and the twins in the kitchen. The girls stood on chairs pulled up to the counter, Evie positioned between them. Luna was already in her church dress, her hair brushed. Not surprisingly, Callie remained in her pajamas and displayed a comical flurry of bedhead.

Evie had her wavy locks up in one of those clippy deals, loose spirals escaping. She wore a pink skirt that hit just below her knees, a white blouse and one of Aunt Martha's floral aprons. Both girls were chattering up a storm. He couldn't remember the last time he'd seen Luna this animated with anyone other than him, Aunt Martha or Lucy.

Watching the three of them interact stirred a longing within him reminiscent of dreams he'd once expected to fulfill with his ex.

Tempting him to think that maybe, just maybe, he could someday experience lasting love. The good Lord knew, the girls needed and deserved a mom. Someone who would listen to their random stories, answer their endless questions and readily invite them close.

Like Evie did.

Why was it, when he'd finally met someone he could see himself falling for, that person was beyond his reach? Too bad there wasn't some way that she could stay.

Unless… He thought back to her phone call from the other

day. While he'd come in on the tail end, he'd caught enough to know New Day had given someone else an assignment she'd wanted. Did that mean she'd have a lapse in employment, once she left here? While he knew little about the in-home care industry, the fact that she was here now seemed to indicate that, along with how much she disliked rural living.

Although he got the impression the hill country was growing on her.

Maybe she wasn't as opposed to ranch life as when she'd first arrived. Would she stay, if asked? If she didn't have anything else lined up after, probably. That would save New Day, and him, the expense of sending someone else down.

Yet, that would merely delay her departure—making it harder for him and the girls to say goodbye once that time came.

Evie turned and caught him watching her. His emotions must've shown in his expression because her cheeks flushed, and her gaze faltered.

"Good morning." She pulled a mug from the cupboard. "Would you like some coffee?"

Face heated, he cleared his throat and went to the sink. "That sounds great. Thank you." He washed his hands, lathering long enough to hog-tie his wayward emotions. He peered at the bowl positioned between her and the girls. "What're y'all making?"

"Crepes." Luna beamed. "With blueberries and whip cream."

"Really?"

She nodded. "Do you know what those are?"

"I've had them once or twice." He glanced around. "Where's Aunt Martha?"

"Lucy picked her up about ten minutes ago." Evie placed a pan on the stovetop. "When she heard your aunt wasn't feeling nauseous, she insisted on treating her to breakfast."

"It's good she's taking time to connect with friends. I know she was bummed about last week's canceled appointment, but I'm glad to see her strength returning. That'll make her treatment this week all the more effective."

Evie looked like she wanted to say something, but Callie hijacked her attention to ask if she could pour the crepe batter into the pan.

He glanced at the clock on the stove. "I best jump in the shower."

By the time he returned, a plate full of crepes that looked like they'd lost a battle against the whip cream centered the table. At least, he assumed crepes sat under the massive white mound.

Twenty minutes later, the girls had washed their hands and faces and Callie had changed. When they arrived at church, they found the lot and sanctuary three-quarters full. Elementary-age kids ran around in the grass, teens gathered in groups of threes and fours, and adults and families filed into pews or conversed in the aisle.

Evie accompanied Monte when he deposited the girls in their classroom. He introduced her to people they encountered there, most of whom gushed with gratitude for her coming to Sage Creek and all she was doing to help his aunt.

He agreed with the sentiment.

Reaching an empty pew, he motioned for Evie to proceed before him.

She slid in, set her purse at her feet and rested her Bible beside her. "It's obvious how much everyone adores your aunt. From what I know about her, with good reason."

His heart swelled as he thought of the legacy his aunt had formed, not just with the girls, which itself was priceless, but also in this community.

"She loves people well." He smiled. "Always has. When I visited her back as a kid, I used to get annoyed by all the folks she'd talk to. Always felt like they carried on for hours—as if hearing to a person talk about their grandkids, or their job, or whatever, was such a terrible thing. Now that's one of the things I admire about her most."

"Listening to someone is one of the best ways to speak value and care."

"They teach you that in your caregiving training?"

She nodded. "Often, when we see people in distress, our first urge is to try to alleviate their pain. By all means, that's a big part of my job—at least for physical discomfort. When it comes to things like sorrow or grief, however, I've found what people need most isn't our answers or so-called solutions but for someone to sit with them in their pain."

"I 'spect you're right."

"I've taken the classes and would've said I'd had plenty of practice walking beside those who hurt. But compared to the people in Sage Creek—" she waved a hand to indicate the other church members "—I'm a novice."

"Can't find this depth of community in a big city, that's for sure."

Her eyes widened for a flash of a second before she frowned and dropped her gaze—almost as if he'd chided her.

Had he offended her in some way? Made her feel like he didn't think she excelled at her job? Or maybe she thought he felt his way of life was superior to what she'd experienced in the city?

Then again, he did. He wouldn't give up this place, the people or his land for any high-rise, no matter how fancy. But that didn't mean he thought anything less of Evie.

He'd simply been encouraged to know she was beginning to see the benefits to country living.

He'd been letting his rebellious heart take the lead, and in the process, had offended the one person he'd been most wanting to impress.

With a sigh, he focused on the front as the choir rose, indicating for everyone else to do the same.

After service, Declan, a guy Monte had talked with a time or two but didn't know well, approached as he was exiting the sanctuary. "Hey." The man had a large Adam's apple, a hooked nose and bony frame that reminded him of the cartoon character Ichabod Crane. "How're you holding up?"

Monte shook the man's hand. "Same ol'." He introduced Declan to Evie, which led to a brief discussion of various jobs through which people traveled the country.

"So," Declan widened his stance and popped his neck. "I heard you're introducing my buddy Ian to bull riding."

"Trying to." Ian had little patience for drills and learning things like body mechanics or ways to avoid getting stomped on—like bolting out of the arena once bucked. Or rather, to reduce the likelihood, because as Monte's mom used to say, it wasn't a matter of *if* a competitor got hurt, but *when*.

He'd known the risks and had taken care to mitigate them. But Ian was showing no such concern.

Declan laughed. "I hear that. Dude's got an invincibility complex if I've ever seen one."

Monte shrugged. While not wanting to talk badly about the kid, there was a lot of truth to that statement. Ian was either rodeo-ignorant or assumed he'd be the only man in bull-riding history not to get injured.

Declan went on to give examples to prove just how out of touch the kid was. "Dude's convinced he's going to become the next Roy Arlington. Just wait until he breaks his jaw or busts his ribs. That'll wisen him up right quick." He shook his head. "Least he's got a great coach. I'm sure you'll steer him straight. Got time for any more students?"

"I don't actually do this on a professional basis. I'm just doing a favor for a family friend." Monte sensed Evie watching him and cast her a sideways glance. Her expression hinted at concern or confusion. Likely the latter, considering her nearly nonexistent exposure to cowboy culture.

The question was, did this conversation, and his way of life, intrigue her? Enough for her to want to stay?

He thought back to his first year of marriage and how hard he'd tried to help Erin love the country as much as he did. He'd ended up with a heap of disappointment, heartache and an ultimatum—grant her a divorce or she'd take the kids with her.

Had he fought her, he would've landed in the same place—without her or custody of the twins, and carrying enough debt from legal fees to about swallow him whole.

He'd gotten so caught up in his thoughts, he'd missed Declan's question. "What's that?"

"Bull riding lessons. You ever think about starting something like that? Could be a real moneymaker."

"I wouldn't even know how to begin."

"Word of mouth goes a long way."

An interesting idea. "I'll think about it." He had a handful of guys he invited out to ride. They helped him get his bulls practice time, and they did the same for the men. But Monte had never charged anyone, or instructed them, for that matter—other than Ian.

And he was a long way from calling the experience a success.

Declan gave a greeting nod to someone who walked past. "My buddies and I would love to come learn a thing or two, if you're open to teaching us. We'd pay, of course. We're going to dig in our spurs in San Antonio this February. Ride or die, as they say." He chuckled. "Consider this an opportunity to help a group of knuckleheads live long enough to swap stories about the bull that nearly did us in."

In other words, they were going to enter the bucking chutes coached or not. And Declan thought Ian was foolish. Monte's parents had said the same about him, when he first started riding. But at least he'd had others to learn from.

A couple with a toddler and a child near the twins' age walked by.

Monte rubbed the back of his neck. "When were you thinking?"

"This weekend be too soon?"

To get anything worth investing that much time into organized, yes. "Taking the girls and a few of my derbies to Dripping Springs."

"The Saturday after?"

"That sounds like a lot of work."

"I'll do the heavy lifting. Gather up the fellas, put flyers around town and such. Probably could even get my buddy at the county paper to write up a community interest piece. All you'd have to do is provide the space and do the coaching."

The idea did sound fun, and like a relatively easy way to boost his shrinking bank account. Plus, an article could help him establish his brand while attracting potential investors.

He shifted his weight from one foot to the other. "You don't think everyone will be too busy to come, with the holidays and all?"

"We could sell it to folks as an early Christmas present."

"You'd do all the leg work?"

"I'd loop my buddies and our girlfriends in to help, but yep."

"All right, then."

"Yeah?" Declan grinned.

"Yep. We can give it a shot." He watched a preschooler dart out of his mom's grasp. That was something his Callie would do. "I best get my girls before their teacher thinks I forgot about them."

"And I better get moving on Sage Creek's first annual winter bull riding clinic."

Monte chuckled. "Let's not get ahead of ourselves here."

He excused himself with a handshake, then, with Evie accompanying him, headed down the hall leading to one of the back classrooms.

"Drake Owens, a local contractor who handles a lot of the church's repairs, built this add-on to make space for the growth of families." The extension had increased the church by nearly one thousand feet. "His wife, Faith, painted the murals." He indicated the cartoonish Bible story scenes decorating the halls. They stopped in the doorway of his daughters' classroom. "The Jenkinses, who owned the local hardware store, donated the carpet."

"That's amazing." Her voice carried a note of admiration. "It sounds like you have a wonderful church family. That's something I really miss."

Sounded like that was another reason she might be willing to stick around. "'Spect it's hard to put down roots when you're always on the move."

Based on the phone conversation he'd overheard, she didn't have anywhere to leave to, at least not for a while. But even if she did stay for the full time he and his family needed, what would happen once Aunt Martha got better?

Seemed the question wasn't *would* Evie be leaving, but *when*. Knowing that should counter any fantasies he had regarding her becoming part of his world. So why did his mind keep envisioning the two of them building a life together?

Because he was hankering for heartache, apparently.

Suppressing a sigh, he turned his attention to the handful of children still waiting to get picked up. Callie and her friend Ramona were sitting in the far corner, creating a structure with magnetic tiles. Luna and a couple other girls were coloring at the table.

"Monte."

He turned at the sound of a familiar voice and smiled at the twins' preschool teacher. "Kate, good to see you."

She greeted Evie.

"Your nephew visiting again?" Monte asked.

She nodded, her gaze shifting to a blond-haired boy who was stacking overturned plastic cups into a tower. "He's staying with me this weekend."

"Ah. Fun."

"And tiring." She laughed. "That kid has more energy than a Boston terrier!"

"Sounds like Callie." He chuckled, then sobered, thinking of her uncharacteristic behavior Friday afternoon. "The girls doing okay at school?"

The way Kate averted her gaze and fiddled with her bracelet concerned him.

His shoulders tensed. "Did something happen? One of the kids giving Callie gruff?"

"Oh, nothing like that."

"Then what is it?"

"Have you ever considered getting her evaluated for ADHD?"

He frowned. "No. Why?"

"I've noticed she likes to fidget. She seems to have difficulty sitting still. And paying attention to details."

"She's an active five-year-old used to having the run of the ranch."

"I understand. I just think it may be a good idea to get her tested. So that, if necessary, we can adapt accordingly."

He relaxed his tight muscles in an attempt to keep his irritation out of his voice. "I appreciate your concern."

Kate was wrong. He loved his daughter's lively personality and inquisitive spirit. Did she get bored easily? Sure. But that was just because her brain was always running. That was a good thing. A gift that would take her far, once maturity balanced her out.

"Auntie Kate." Her nephew broke the awkward silence stretching between them.

Monte used the opportunity to excuse himself. He thanked the Sunday school teacher and crossed the room, with Evie, to where Luna sat drawing.

"Hey, kiddo." He squatted down to her eye level. "What've you got there?"

She'd drawn a colorful picture of a woman standing in front of what resembled a stove or counter, a child on each side.

Luna beamed up at him. "This is my thank You art. God takes care of me just like He took care of the hungry widow the prophet Elijah lived with." Turning her smile to Evie, she relayed the basic details, with slight error.

He smiled "I see. Like Aunt Martha and Ms. Evie cook food for us."

Luna nodded. "In the story, the widow's son died. That was really sad and scary. But God brought him back to life."

A lump lodged in his throat as he considered how hard and confusing Aunt Martha's cancer must feel to the twins. But he was also grateful to know they were clinging to hope in their all-powerful Savior.

Luna handed her paper to Evie. "It's for you. I'm glad God sent you to take care of us. Before, Daddy was tired and cranky, but he's happy now. Aunt Martha, too."

Moisture filled Evie's eyes as she accepted the heartfelt gift. "Thank you. I love it."

Luna stood and wrapped her arms around Evie, cheek to her belly.

Seeing them embrace flooded Monte with emotion.

His daughter was right. He'd been stressed and over-whelmed the past few months, worrying about his aunt, his girls, the ranch. Before Tracy came and in the space between her dismissal and Evie's arrival, he'd barely had time to cram a sandwich in his face, let alone be an attentive father to his girls. When they most needed nurturing, he'd been distracted or easily irritated.

But he also had to admit to the truth of Luna's assessment regarding how things had changed. After what felt like a long stretch of inner angst and gloom, he *was* happy. These days he regularly sprang out of bed well before the sun rose. And then rushed about to finish his morning chores so that he could get back for breakfast with Aunt Martha and the girls.

And Evie.

How often had he found excuses to pop into the house numerous times each day, to see her smile, catch a whiff of her soft floral scent, and in some way to bring out her sweet, almost musical laugh?

Despite his good sense, he found himself once again thinking about what life might look like, were Evie to stay. Along with how he might convince her to do that.

Yes, she was a city girl, and about as unaccustomed to ranching life as a newborn calf was to the bucking chutes. But he'd also watched those same bulls come alive in the very places they'd once avoided.

He tensed as his thoughts shifted to his ex-wife, but he gave himself a mental shake. It was true Erin had captured his heart then trampled it in the ground, abandoning him and the girls. But he'd never sought God's will like he learned to do once she left. Nor had she. If they had prayed more—for each other and their marriage—things might've turned out differently.

Regardless, the Good Lord had brought Evie to Sage Creek. She was the clearest answer to prayer he'd experienced in some time. He'd always assumed God brought her here for a season. But what if He was doing an even greater work?

What if He was teaching Monte to trust once again?

And maybe even to allow himself to believe he could find someone to spend the rest of his days with.

Chapter Eleven

The next morning, Callie fussed about not wanting to go to school, then did so again the day after, and the next. Come Thursday, she refused to get out of bed, declaring that she was already smart enough. When this didn't work, she said she didn't feel well. When pressed, however, she named enough "ailments" to confirm Evie's suspicions—the child was fibbing.

Martha entered and sat on the edge of Callie's bed. "What's wrong, dear?" Dressed and hair done, she looked livelier than Evie had yet seen her.

Martha's time with her friend had done her good. Evie needed to encourage her to go out more often.

Callie clutched her blanket beneath her chin as if ready to fight for it. "I don't want to go to school."

Martha smoothed the child's hair out of her face. "But your friends and Ms. Vargas will miss you."

She shook her head. "My teacher doesn't like me."

"Don't be silly. Of course, she does," Evie said.

Callie's frown deepened. "She likes Luna better."

"That's only because you get in trouble so much," Luna said from across the room where she sat putting on pink, lace-topped socks.

Martha's expression turned stern. "Seems the solution, then, is to stop misbehaving."

"That's what I try to do," Callie whined.

"I suggest you try harder." Martha stood and planted a fist

on her hip. "And get yourself up and moving. Otherwise, you won't have time for breakfast, and I'm pretty sure we can talk the chef into making chocolate chip pancakes." She shot Evie a playful smile.

Bribing them with food. Smart.

She nodded. "With whip cream."

Both girls perked up at this and darted for the door.

Martha stopped them. "Not until you make your bed, you don't."

As expected, Luna readily obeyed, and Callie whined. But she must've complied, because by the time Evie poured batter into a heated frying pan, both girls were playing happily in the living room.

Monte walked in a few minutes later, stopping first to see the twins. "Y'all about ready for school?"

Luna informed him they hadn't eaten yet, along with what was on the menu.

"So that's what smells so good. How'd you finagle that?" His teasing tone carried a hint of tenderness.

"Callie threw a fit," Luna said.

"Did not."

"Did so."

"You're a tattletale."

"Am not."

"Yes, huh. And a stupid head."

"No. You are. I'm smarter than you."

"I'm stronger and faster."

"Enough." Monte's firm voice silenced them. "Why don't you girls watch some cartoons while you're waiting?"

A moment later, the television came on.

Monte ambled into the kitchen shaking his head. "Those two. Best friends one minute, bitter enemies the next." He grabbed a mug from the cupboard and poured himself some coffee. "What set them off this morning?"

Evie relayed Callie's attempts to stay in bed along with what Luna had said about their teacher.

He released a breath. "That child. She can be a stubborn one. She's also prone to forget her manners, especially when she's got words firing through her brain but it's not her turn to speak. I sure hope she's not being disrespectful to Ms. Vargas."

Evie bit her lip, remembering his conversation with the teacher the day before. One to which he hadn't seemed that receptive. Most likely, he'd been caught off guard. That probably hadn't been the best time to talk with a father about his daughter's misbehavior.

While Evie didn't have experience with learning disabilities or anything, what the teacher had said made sense.

"Have you given Ms. Vargas's question any more thought?" She flipped a pancake over.

"Which was?"

"About getting Callie tested for ADHD."

He snorted. "The child's fine. Maybe more active than most, sure. But what would you expect? She's had five years of chasing after the dogs, climbing trees and splashing about in the creek. She'll acclimate to her new environment soon enough."

She should probably let this go. These weren't her kids, nor did she have any business giving parenting advice. But she'd seen the pain one of her closest friends, growing up, had experienced, fighting her way through school. For years, she assumed she was stupid while her parents called her lazy. Come to find out, her difficulties came from dyslexia.

Grabbing a platter from the cupboard, Evie took in a slow, deep breath. Exhaling, she faced him. "But if she does have a learning disability, wouldn't you want to know? So that you can help her get the resources she needs?"

"You implying I don't know my own daughter?" She hadn't heard such hostility in his voice since the day of the mud incident. "Or do you just think you know better how to raise them?"

Her stomach felt queasy. "I'm sorry. I shouldn't have said anything."

"You're right about that." He deposited his mug on the counter with a clank and stomped off.

Although his mood appeared to have improved by the time he returned to breakfast, he seemed more interested in eating than conversation. Seemed maybe her statement had hit a nerve.

He was probably just stressed about his aunt's appointment today. Considering his family's circumstances, his reaction hadn't been abnormal. Most people struggled to manage their emotions in these situations.

Was his aunt's condition and all the uncertainty related to it triggering because he'd lost his wife? Regardless of why their marriage had ended, he had grieved her twice, first when she broke things off, then again when, upon her death, her absence became irrevocably permanent.

He grabbed his plate and stood. "I'll walk the girls to the bus stop. Y'all can leave for Houston now, if you'd like. Give yourself some leeway, in case you hit traffic."

Evie made eye contact with Martha. "On the way, do you want to swing by that bakery you told me about? The one with the ginormous slices of caramel-apple-spice-cheesecake?"

"I want some!" Callie pushed her half-finished breakfast aside as if wanting to save room for the heavenly treat. "Can I, please? I'll mind my manners and won't give Ms. Vargas any trouble." When her aunt didn't respond, she added, "I'll clean my room, too, without giving you lip. And the chicken coop."

Mouth twitching toward a smile, Monte raised an eyebrow. "All that for a bit of dessert? Seems like a fair trade to me." He tossed his aunt a wink.

Frowning, she dropped her gaze and began gathering the dirty dishes. "We'll see."

This led to more begging, pleading and whining from Callie, which Monte silenced with a warning that she'd get nothing but broccoli if she kept it up.

"I'll take the girls to school," he said. "So y'all can get a head start on traffic." He opened the door for the girls. "No dawdling, now."

They shrugged on their backpacks and shuffled out, Callie slumping like she'd lost an entire year of recess privileges.

Evie laughed. "That child sure is food motivated, huh?"

Martha sighed. "That complicates things."

Helping clean up, Evie furrowed her brow. "What do you mean?"

"Never mind." She placed the last of the used silverware into the dishwasher, slipped her purse strap over her shoulder and smoothed a hand over her up-done hair. "Shall we?"

"Yep. Just give me a sec to grab your medical binder."

Ten minutes later, they were passing by Monte and the girls who were waiting for the bus, and then they were en route to Houston.

The fields stretching on either side of them blurred into endless streams of green periodically accented with dilapidated barns, two-story farmhouses and towering grain silos. They came alongside a train rumbling down the tracks to their left bearing the marks of red, orange and green graffiti.

Aunt Martha pulled papers from her purse. The first one contained printed directions.

Evie tossed her a smile. "I plugged the address to the treatment facility into my phone's GPS."

"That's not where this'll take us." She showed her the second page, a map. "You ever been to San Marcos?"

Evie shook her head.

"You're going to turn left on Texas 71. Heading west. Should be coming up in a mile or so."

Evie looked at her phone held in the dashboard mount. "You mean east?"

"Nope."

"But…" Glancing at she papers again, she caught the to and from locations printed at the top. "Your appointment's at ten, right?" Had she entered it wrong into her calendar? Even so, this was supposed to be an all-day thing, which meant they didn't have time for an out-of-the way pit stop.

"I canceled."

"What? When?" Was her primary care physician still concerned with her blood count? It would've been nice if someone had let Evie know.

"A few days ago."

But why hadn't she told her? Or Monte, for that matter, because he thought they were heading to Houston.

Evie pulled onto the shoulder and parked. "What's going on?"

Martha sighed. "I can't do this anymore. I won't waste what little time I have left with Monte and the girls holed up in bed."

She could understand Martha's discouragement, especially considering her fatigue and extreme dizziness the week before. Followed by a brief reprieve when, as far as Evie could tell, she'd regained some of her energy and maybe even a bit of joy. And she still had a long, challenging journey ahead.

"I know this is hard," Evie said. "But you can do this. You're strong and brave, and you've got a lot of people standing with you."

Martha frowned. "Look, I know you mean well, but I've made up my mind. I'm done fighting. I want to start living, while I still have life left in my bones."

Evie didn't know what to say. Besides, Martha probably had considered every aspect of her options, ten times over. She knew what stopping treatment meant.

Monte would be devastated. Martha knew that more so than anyone. This couldn't have been an easy decision.

But it was hers, and hers alone, to make.

They sat in silence for a moment with cool air blowing through the dashboard vents and the hum of an occasional vehicle passing by.

"You ever driven along a hill country highway in spring?" Martha asked.

She shook her head.

"It's a sight, let me tell you. All those wildflowers dancing in the sun. Splashing the surrounding countryside with vibrant color."

"I've seen pictures of long, wide rows of bluebonnets stretching as far as the eye can see. They're gorgeous. They're the state flower, right?"

Martha nodded. "They're often the first to bloom each spring. Folks say that's when the sky falls on Texas. Seems fitting to me, only I'd swap the word *heaven* for sky." She smiled. "Those delicate yet hardy flowers remind us of the God who brings beauty and life following the longest, most barren winters."

"I love that."

After a while, Martha produced a handwritten list from her purse and gave it to Evie.

"What's this?"

"My bucket list."

She read the items. Cruise Canyon Lake's River Road. Visit the Sugar Shack in Bastrop. Take a glass boat tour. She glanced up. "This is a lot more than a one-day excursion."

"As the saying goes, Rome wasn't built—or a bucket list accomplished—in one day."

Only problem—Evie wouldn't be around to drive her much longer. That meant, once she left, Martha would need to have this same conversation with the caregiver that came after her.

"Enough about that." Martha took her list back and returned it, folded, to her purse. "I'm ready for that glass boat tour. Followed by the biggest ice cream cone I can stomach."

"Think we should swing by a local bakery? To get something for the girls?"

"May be wise. Our little Callie probably will be dreaming of cakes and pies all day. May even have half the house tidied up by the time we get back."

"And her entire apple eaten."

"Oh, lands." Martha feigned an eye roll. "We certainly can't let that go unrewarded. The girl may decide to boycott all fruits and vegetables for the remainder of her childhood."

"What about Monte? You going to tell him?"

Martha's gaze dropped to her hands. "When the time is right. And I get my courage."

Evie couldn't imagine how hard this was for her. But she also hoped Martha would make good on that promise, because the thought of keeping this from him made her feel ill.

Yet, she had no choice in the matter. Martha was her patient, and as such, she had the right to privacy, a right Evie was legally bound to uphold.

Either way, Monte would be heartbroken. Maybe even blame her, if not hate her. Knowing there wasn't anything she could do about that didn't make her feel any better.

On Friday, Monte loaded three of his bulls into a trailer and gave his ranch hands, Travis and Jesse, last-minute reminders. He also verified, again, that Lucy still planned to stay with his aunt while he was away at the Christmas rodeo. He would've felt much better had he been able to wait until she arrived, but he needed to pick the girls up from school and get on the road.

Sliding into his truck beside Evie, he couldn't contain his grin.

"That mischievous look on your face tells me you've pulled a prank on your guys."

He chuckled and shifted into gear. "Just thinking about how excited the girls must've been today. It's been a while since I've taken them to the rodeo."

Aunt Martha had been right. This would be a memorable weekend for them all.

In his case, potentially too memorable. The more time he spent with Evie, the more he wanted to be around her.

Suppressing a sigh, he turned onto the two-lane highway leading into town. "Listen, I'm sorry I was such a bear yesterday, when you suggested Callie might have ADHD." After a bit of a restless night trying to decipher why he'd acted like he had, he realized his frustration had nothing to do with Evie, or anything Kate Vargas had said, for that matter.

"No big deal." She offered him the sweetest, most genuine smile, as if she'd already forgotten what a jerk he'd been.

That almost made him feel worse.

He'd filtered her and Kate's words through his parental insecurities, taking a simple suggestion as a statement against him as a father. Part of him felt like he should've been the first to detect any learning disability the child might have. Another side determined that Callie wouldn't have one at all, had he been less wrapped up in the ranch.

Eventually, common sense won out, overpowering his defensiveness with gratitude that God had placed caring and attentive adults in the twins' lives.

For now.

The fact that he'd known, from the moment Evie arrived, that she wouldn't stay long, didn't make remembering that now any easier.

The parking lot at the preschool was nearly full.

"Want me to hop out and get them?" Evie reached for her door.

He glanced at the trailer hitched to his truck. "Sure would be a lot easier than trying to finagle this beast."

With a quick nod, she jumped out and strolled down the sidewalk and toward the building. Ten minutes later, she returned, holding the girls' hands, unfiltered, unconstrained joy radiating from each of their faces.

He wasn't the only one who'd come to adore the woman. That meant he wouldn't be the only one who'd feel gut-punched when she left.

Convince her to stay.

The thought landed so strong and clear, he wanted to believe it came from God—because then he could hold it like a promise. But it was far more likely the notion came from within his renegade heart.

And yet, could he entice Evie to change her plans and remain in Sage Creek—forever?

Was that what he wanted? Bigger question—could he, the girls and the ranch be what *she* wanted?

He got out as they drew near and greeted each of his daughters with an off-the-ground hug. "Y'all ready for some mutton busting?"

"Yeah!" Their enthusiasm sent a rush of warmth through him.

"You best get in then, because this wrangler's ready to go." Helping the girls climb in, he winked at Evie, delighted by the sparkle in her eyes and the slight flush in her cheeks.

Once everyone was strapped in, he veered around the vehicles idling in front of him and through the adjacent neighborhood. As they continued toward Dripping Springs, homes gave way to pastureland dotted with longhorns and clusters of leafless trees.

Initially, the girls chatted about everything from kettle corn and walking tacos to barrel racing and how long they planned to stay on top of their sheep. Unfortunately, Callie soon grew bored and began asking, repeatedly, how much longer before they arrived.

"Ten minutes less than when you asked last time, Cowpoke." Evie made eye contact with him. "You're patient."

The admiration in her tone made him sit a mite taller. "I

figure her questions stem from her excitement. And frustration with sitting still for any length of time. That girl came into the world looking for a challenge to conquer and a race to win."

"I love that about her."

He did, too, and it touched him to know that Evie saw the strength, the spark, in what others might deem a weakness.

"I have an idea." She twisted in her seat to look at the twins. "Have you ever played the alphabet game?" When they said they hadn't, she explained it to them.

They immediately began calling out the letters, starting with *A*, in various license plates and road signs.

He joined in.

By the time they reached the rodeo, they'd played four rounds, along with "I spy." Evie had also led them in a game she called "Add and pass", where she started a story, and they each took turns adding to it.

He pulled into a large gravel lot filled with horse and cattle trailers, pickups and RVs, then waited his turn to back into the appropriate loading chute. "Once I get these fellas taken care of, I'll drive you and the girls to the regular entrance. Figured you might like to catch a behind-the-scenes glimpse."

He checked the time on the dash. They'd arrived plenty early for this size of a shindig. "Some guys bring their bulls out the night before, to get them acclimated and whatnot." He would've, too, had this been a larger rodeo or PBR event.

Evie took everything in with wide eyes. "This is so cool. I'm really looking forward to this. Thank you for taking me."

His breath hitched. He cleared his throat and gave one firm nod. "Couldn't let you leave Texas without experiencing a bit of cowboy culture."

He'd rather she not leave at all.

Seeing the almost childlike wonder in her expression made him think, if this weekend went well, he stood a chance at stopping that from happening.

Chapter Twelve

Evie took the girls to the Coyote Arena to check them in for their event while Monte did whatever it was he needed to do with his bulls. The air smelled like dust, kettle corn and animals. People, most of them dressed in country attire, filled the bleachers and streamed up and down the stairs.

With an hour to spare, she and the girls left to explore the fairgrounds.

They returned with lemonade and funnel cakes to find Monte waiting near the arena entrance. "Do I get some of that?" he teased Luna.

The child's face fell as she looked from him to her treat, which was large enough to give her a bellyache twice over.

Shoulders slumped, she nodded and reluctantly raised her snack.

"You can eat your own, thank you very much." With feigned annoyance, Evie held out her plate, topped with two funnel cakes dusted with a healthy dose of powdered sugar.

Monte grinned. "Thanks for thinking of me. And my stomach."

Heat rushed to her face at the truth of his statement. She *had* been thinking of him, and not only when standing at the food stand. Her thoughts turned to him much too often. Worse, there'd been numerous times when, instead of fighting them, she'd let various fantasies play out of the two of them together, sitting in the gazebo, her nestled against his strong chest, watching the sun set. Or riding horses across the pasture, or sipping coffee on the porch while Luna colored and Callie played tug-of-war with Max.

Callie grimaced as Monte secured her helmet onto her head. "It's hot and heavy and itchy."

Monte shot her a stern look. "No helmet, no riding."

Her torso deflated as she released an exasperated breath. But then she turned to Evie with a wide grin. "Will you watch me?"

"I wouldn't miss that for the world." She turned to Luna. "You, either."

The child's face lit with such joy, Evie couldn't help but give her a quick squeeze. Funny, prior to coming to Sage Creek, she'd felt certain she wasn't ready for kids. Hadn't been entirely sure she ever would be.

Now she found herself looking forward to the day when she had a family of her own.

When the time came, Monte accompanied the girls into the bucking chute while Evie watched from the bleachers.

The announcer proclaimed Callie's name, age and from where she came, as she burst out of the gate, arms and legs wrapped around the sheep, her head turned and cheek pressed into the thick gray wool. She stayed on for six and a half seconds. Based on the enthusiasm of the announcer and the crowd, that must've been good. Although Luna lasted just shy of five, her bright smile indicated she was pleased with herself.

Both girls received ribbons they proudly displayed to Evie.

"Way to go!" She gave them each a high five. "I knew you'd rock it. Both of you."

With a hand on each of the girls' shoulders, Monte seemed to stand a bit taller. "That's my little wranglers, all right."

"What's next?" Evie asked.

"Bull riding's always the last event. That's the rodeo director's way of making sure people stick around." He laughed. "You ever seen horse cutting?"

She shook her head. "But it sounds interesting."

"This way." He led them out of the Coyote Arena and into the open air, then stopped. "Mind if I call one of my ranch hands right quick? Make sure they haven't encountered—or created—any fires I need to walk them through?"

"Not at all."

They migrated past a handful of food booths decked out in Christmas lights to an empty picnic table.

With a foot on the bench, Monte pulled his phone from his back pocket and tapped the screen. "Hey, Travis. How're things going?" He paused. "Sounds great. Did Lucy make it over okay?" His eyebrows shot up. "Really. That's good to hear." He smiled. "I agree with you there." He straightened to standing. "Holler at me if you need anything."

He ended the call and looked at Evie with an adoration that about stole her breath. And her heart. "Good news, I take it?"

"Seems Aunt Martha's been busy. Brought the fellas fried chicken and homemade coleslaw for supper then headed out with Lucy for ladies' bunco night at the church. According to my ranch hand, looking more alive than he'd seen her in some time."

"Yeah?" Her stomach soured as she thought about the reason for his aunt's increased energy. "That's awesome."

"It is, thanks to you. To say you've been an answer to prayers would be an understatement. With you by her side, she'll beat this cancer, for sure." His eyes deepened in intensity. "Say you'll stay?"

Her heart squeezed with equal parts hope and concern. "What?"

"I didn't mean to eavesdrop, but I assume from the conversation I overheard the other day, you don't have another assignment lined up for when you leave here."

"Not yet." That did concern her.

"Doesn't make sense to me for your company to send some-one else out, when you're already here, and doing such a great job. I'd like to think that maybe country living has grown on you, least enough to entice you to stick around through the end of my aunt's treatment."

And when he learned, according to his aunt, that day had already arrived?

It made her nauseous, keeping something so big from him, especially considering his high hopes. But she didn't have a choice.

Would he understand that, once his aunt told him about her decision?

Regardless, he was right about one thing. It didn't make sense to ask another caregiver to come all this way, poten-tially costing her an assignment elsewhere, only to learn the Bowmans didn't need her after all.

"I think it's wise to keep things as they are for now."

"Meaning, tell New Day not to send your replacement?"

She nodded. Once his aunt told him about her decision, there'd be no need for the company to send anyone else. This way, if Martha delayed her revelation, whoever was supposed to come out next could find another assignment.

His grin widened. "Awesome." He pulled her into his strong arms, his heartbeat thudding against her ear, and she melted against him.

Apparently, the embrace surprised him as much as it had her, because they simultaneously stiffened and pulled apart, his cheeks as red as hers felt.

Taking half a step back, he cleared his throat and gazed toward a red building with white trim. "Let's go see us some horses."

With a deep breath to center her tumbling thoughts and

slow her accelerated pulse, she followed, wishing things could be different.

That she truly could stay as more than a temporary caregiver, not that Monte had asked for that. But the way he'd looked at her a moment ago, as if she was the most beautiful woman he'd encountered, made her think maybe, just maybe that was what he wanted.

Would that change once he learned of his aunt's decision—and that she hadn't talked her out of it?

Monte had just finished loading up his bulls and was about to text Evie when a tall, pot-bellied man with gray hair and mustache approached. He wore a black cowboy hat, a collared, blue shirt, dark jeans and boots that looked fresh out of the box. The man's swagger suggested he was someone with money and influence.

When the guy reached the truck, Monte lowered his window and greeted him with a nod.

"You Mr. Bowman, from Bowman's Rough Stock Ranch?"

Monte sat up taller. "I am."

"You got some mighty fine bulls."

"Thank you."

"Your wife said this was Jackhammer's first competition?"

His what? His shoulders tensed as an image of Erin, his former wife, came to mind. But then he smiled. The guy must be talking about Evie.

His wife. Monte liked the sound of that. As if that were even an option.

Could it be? Maybe, if she stayed through Aunt Martha's treatment, and he managed to capture her heart during that time. Those were some serious ifs—a definite challenge, but not impossible.

He corralled his thoughts back to the present. "With a rider, yes, sir." Monte had entered him in a handful of futurities, during which his performance had been hit-or-miss. The animal hadn't been much more consistent with riders brought onto the ranch for practice.

Monte hadn't been expecting much different tonight. He'd been pleasantly surprised.

The man eyed his trailer, then refocused on Monte. "I'm Cord Mariluch."

Monte introduced himself as the two shook hands, although clearly the guy already knew who he was. The name of his ranch, at least.

Cord rested a hand on his large, silver-and-turquoise belt buckle. "I hear you're looking for investors."

A jolt shot through him. "Yes, sir."

Had Evie been acting as salesperson while watching from the stands? The thought warmed him and made him feel like they were a team—something he'd never felt with his ex. Oh, Erin had said she supported him, in the beginning, anyway.

But she'd bailed before his first homebred bulls started practicing with dummies.

Prior to the girls learning to potty train, count to ten, or form their letters.

And he'd thought her the loyal type. Boy, had she fooled him.

Cord widened his stance. "You got any information on you?"

"I do." He grabbed a file folder with pictures and details on some of his best bulls.

The man studied each page, then flipped back to the first, where Monte had printed his phone number, email and website. He asked a few more questions, including how long Monte had been in the bucking bulls business and how many bulls he had available for partnership.

"I'll give all this some thinking on. Can I keep this?" He raised the folder.

"Please do."

Cord nodded and started to walk away.

"Mind if I reach out to you in a week or so?" Experience told him, an interest was more apt to turn into a sale when he followed up later.

Cord turned back around. "Sure." He handed Monte a business card, tipped his hat and strolled away.

Thank You, Lord. While this wasn't a check in hand, it was a great lead. A wealthy investor paired with a bull as intelligent and athletic as Jackhammer was looking to be would go a long way toward establishing the Bowman name in the bucking bull business.

He reached for his phone to call Evie, then paused. When a potential blessing fell his way, she'd been the first person he wanted to tell.

That was how much she'd come to mean to him. And if he couldn't talk her into staying?

That wasn't an option.

He shot her a text to let her know he was heading her way, even more anxious to hear what she thought of his bulls than he was to tell her about the potential investor.

She climbed into his truck carrying the floral scent that always set him off-kilter, her eyes bright in the dim overhead light of his cab.

She handed him a hot dog doused with ketchup, mustard and jalapeños, just the way he liked it.

He grinned. "How'd you know?"

"The girls told me."

He glanced back at them through his rearview mirror. Smears of ketchup and mustard on their faces, they looked droopy-eyed but content. "Y'all did good."

Evie snapped on her seat belt. "You're not going to believe this, but I met a guy who invests in bucking bulls. Callie overheard him talking on the phone to someone about Jackhammer, told him he belonged to her daddy, the 'best and strongest and smartest cowboy in all of Texas.'"

He laughed. "Did she, now?"

Evie nodded. "He seemed interested and started asking me questions, none of which I had answers to, unfortunately."

"Well, you came off knowledgeable enough for him to think we were married."

"What?" Her eyes widened, and he wondered if he'd see a blush on her cheeks, if his cab wasn't so dark. "I guess that makes sense, me sitting with your girls and all."

"So, what'd you think? Was this what you expected?" He motioned toward the fairgrounds.

"Better." She smiled. "And I was much relieved to overhear a couple of guys talking about how the bulls are treated. That lady I met at the twins' party made it seem like they were tortured into bucking."

He snorted. "Hardly. An animal in pain doesn't perform any better than an injured human would."

"I suppose not."

He turned onto a winding country road. Luna fell asleep less than ten miles out. That was about the time Callie's energetic chattering began to slow before dying entirely.

He glanced at her in the rearview mirror. "Out cold."

Evie craned her neck to glance behind her. "I'm not surprised, with all the jumping up and down those two did. They were your personal cheerleaders and made sure everyone in the vicinity knew it."

"Luna included?"

She nodded.

"Wow. She must've been pretty excited, for it to overpower her shyness like that."

"They're both quite proud of their father."

A lump lodged in his throat. "Hope they always feel that way."

"I'm sure they will. You're a great dad."

The lump grew. He cleared his throat to hide the rush of emotion her honest admiration caused. "Thanks. And for coming. It meant the world to the girls."

"I had a wonderful time." He could hear the smile in her voice. Could picture it on her delicate, pink lips.

"Does that mean country life has grown on you?"

"Maybe." She was silent for a moment, but it didn't feel awkward or like either of them needed to fill it. "Callie told me you used to be quite the bull rider. Better than any of the cowboys competing tonight."

He chuckled. "That child can spin a tale."

"Were you any good?"

"I made some money. And broke some bones."

"Is that why you stopped?"

He frowned. "Nope." He didn't want to ruin a nice night talking about his ex. "Like my pops used to tell me, whenever he heard I was heading out to another rodeo, I'm either too stubborn or too stupid for my own good. Figure I'm a bit of both."

"You a born risk-taker, too?"

"Not really. If you're asking what got me started, I'll come clean now and say it was for the ladies. Thought sliding into the bucking chute made me more of a man. I also hoped to win some easy money."

"From what I saw tonight, seems to me there are a lot easier ways to make a living."

"I quickly found out just how right you are. If you're not any good or draw some exceptionally rank bulls, the sport can cost a pretty penny—by way of hospital bills."

That was one of his ex's most frequent arguments. She was convinced it was only a matter of time before he got seriously stomped on, potentially, to his death. Her concerns weren't entirely unfounded.

He turned onto the highway and set his cruise control. "What attracted you to the traveling health care industry?"

"The sense of adventure. Initially, it was only supposed to be for a year—to visit a few places, meet interesting people, try fun foods. Not that I don't enjoy caregiving. I do. I just didn't think I'd be up for living out of a suitcase as long as I did."

She'd changed her plans once. Would she consider Monte and the girls reason enough to do so again?

She'd also spoken in the past tense. Did that mean she no longer enjoyed hoofing it from one place to the next? "And now?"

"What's next, you mean?"

He nodded.

"I'm still trying to figure that out."

He liked hearing that. "You thinking you may change careers?"

"I don't know." She sighed. "I love working with people. Years ago, my grandmother had a heart attack that resulted in a double bypass. We were all scared at how close we'd come to losing her. Some of the hospital staff treated her like she was nothing but a task on their to-do list."

"I hate to say this, but I know exactly what you mean."

"But there was this one guy. The night nurse. He was amazing. It was like he carried supernatural tranquility with him. Changed the atmosphere in the room simply by entering it. When I learned later that he was a Christ-follower, it made sense. He brought the Prince of peace with him, simply by showing up. I wanted to be like him. To bring hope and encouragement to people in the most difficult and frightening seasons of their life, especially."

He placed his hand on hers. "You've done that for us. And I cannot express how grateful I am."

She seemed to be shutting down. She pulled her hand away.

"I didn't say that to pressure you into staying. I'd never do that." While he'd do anything to keep her in Sage Creek, with him, he wanted her to want that, too. If he pestered her into making a decision her heart wasn't set on, she'd come to resent him.

Erin had taught him that, and he wasn't looking for a repeat lesson.

Silence stretched between them.

Sensing her watching him, he cast her a sideways glance. "Why do I get the feeling you're fretting about something?" Was his question too direct? In light of their conversation, and the fact that she'd already withdrawn from him, probably.

"I know it's not any of my business, but what happened with you and the twins' mom?"

He tensed, and the desire to deflect traveled all the way down into his gut. But the fact that she asked indicated she was contemplating building a relationship with him. Made sense she'd want to know why his marriage had failed.

He rubbed the back of his neck. "Erin and I hung with the same friend group in high school. I was a football player. She was a cheerleader, and once I finally convinced her to give me a chance, we spent a lot of time together riding the bus to and from games. I fooled myself into thinking she liked me for myself. But she was only interested in my persona."

"A status thing?"

"Maybe so. Back then, I wasn't very future-minded and hadn't a clue what direction to head. So, when she got accepted to a Texas university, I followed. I took agricultural classes and made friends with some local cowboys. I'd done some riding prior, but that's when I really fell in love with the sport. At first, Erin was thrilled. With the line-dancing, country-music side of things."

"She lost interest in what became for you a driving passion?"

"Exactly. For her, the lifestyle was nothing but a passing phase. As was I. So, when life got tough, she left. I tried to fight for her. Was even willing to go to counseling, but she wasn't interested. I later learned she'd fallen for someone else. Less than a year after, she and her boyfriend died in a car accident."

"I'm sorry."

He shrugged. "It's in the past."

For a time, Erin had left him jaded to love.

Then Evie had arrived with her sweet smile, soft laugh and engaging personality and had started chiseling away at the protective walls barricading his heart.

He fully intended to do whatever possible to make her fall for him as hard as he'd fallen for her.

While he hadn't yet figured out how to do that, one thing he knew for sure—were she to leave, he'd never recover.

Chapter Thirteen

Monday morning, Callie was as reluctant to get ready for preschool as she had been the week prior. Evie sat beside her on the bed and rubbed the child's back in slow, circular motions. "I understand how you feel, sweetie."

"You didn't like school when you were my age, either?"

"I was a bit older, but yeah. I went through a period where I was nervous about going."

"Cuz you were stupid?"

Her heart clenched. "Oh, sweetie, you are *not* stupid. You're bright, creative and full of life. You're just learning when to let your energy loose and when to rein it in."

"Like Dad had to teach Kit Kat?"

She frowned. "Who's that?"

"His friend's horse. His old owners didn't take good care of him or ride him or nothing. So he thought he could do whatever he wanted, even if it wasn't good for him and made people not want him anymore." Sorrow filled her eyes. "That's how Ms. Vargas feels about me."

"That's not true."

"Yuh-huh. She says she likes me, but I can tell she doesn't."

"Because she corrects you?"

She nodded.

Evie offered a gentle smile. "She's a teacher. That's her job. And you're a kid, which means you're going to make mistakes."

Callie sighed. "I make a lot of them."

"I wouldn't expect any different."

"More than Luna."

"She's got her struggles, too."

"Like what?"

Evie wasn't looking to bash one child to make the other feel better. "What's important is that Ms. Vargas loves you. So do I."

The child sat straighter. "You do?"

Evie's heart squeezed at the realization of just how true her statement was. She nodded.

"So do I, Cowpoke." Monte entered smelling like leather, citrus and the faint aroma of hay.

His gaze shifted to Evie, and the intensity in his eyes suggested he felt the same about her.

Dare she believe it?

If so, then what? She thought back to his request that she stay—through his aunt's treatment, which technically had already ended. Not only was that far from a declaration of love, but whatever fondness he did feel for her could easily sour once he learned the truth.

Callie crossed her arms, her bottom lip poked out. "I still don't want to go."

"Unfortunately, you don't—"

Evie interrupted him with a forceful cough and shake of her head.

He furrowed his brow but remained quiet.

She smoothed the hair out of Callie's face. "How about if I talk to Ms. Vargas? I have some ideas I think may help you feel less...confined."

"Like what?"

"Let me chat with her first." She didn't want to plant hope she had no power to fulfill or to inadvertently pit the child against her teacher.

"What if she says no?"

"Then we'll figure something else out. But I can promise you this, Ms. Vargas wants you to enjoy school as much as possible."

"How do you know?"

"From seeing all the decorations, toys and sensory stations she's got in her classroom."

"I like the manipulatives area. That's what she calls the building blocks and marble pipes and stuff."

"See?"

Callie nodded.

"Do we have a deal?"

She gave a slight shrug.

"I'll take that as a yes." Evie shot Monte a grin. Her breath caught to see him watching her with the same intensity as before.

Maybe even a look of adoration.

She stood, suddenly shy. And saddened at the thought of losing the man she'd fallen so hard for, despite all her efforts to remain emotionally detached.

Hand on her hip, she faced Callie. "How about you get dressed while I make you and your sister chocolate chip pancakes?"

"With bunny ears?"

She laughed. "Sure."

She exited the room. Monte followed close behind.

Aunt Martha was already in the kitchen stirring something in a large ceramic bowl. Beside this lay a package of grated cheese. Diced mushrooms, onions and tomatoes waited on a nearby cutting board.

"What's all this?" Monte greeted her with a kiss to the cheek.

"Figured, with all of the high-sugared breakfasts you've stomached of late, it was time I made one of your favorites."

"Omelets?"

She beamed at him. "Yep. With bacon and hot buttery toast."

He looked between her and Evie with a sheepish expression.

Aunt Martha's brow furrowed. "What's wrong?"

Evie told her about the deal she'd struck with Callie.

"Well." Aunt Martha eyed her fresh chopped vegetables. "I guess that simply means we'll serve both. You can bring your ranch hands whatever we don't finish."

"Great plan." He poured himself a cup of coffee then leaned back against the counter, one foot crossed over the other. He made eye contact with Evie. "Mind if I join you when you take the girls to school?"

To the contrary, as the sudden flutter that swept through her midsection verified. "Of course not. They are your children, after all."

Would he take her gentle teasing as flirting?

Did she want him to?

She suppressed a sigh. This was exactly why she'd never been a fan of dating. She stank at it. Whereas some women came off sweet and demure, she excelled at being painfully awkward.

He alleviated her insecurity with some playful teasing of his own, and by the time they were ready to leave, she no longer felt tempted to hide behind a mound of dirty dishes.

His cell rang as he stepped onto the porch, and he glanced at the screen. His eyebrows shot up, his lips twitching toward a hint of a smile. Holding up a finger to Evie, he answered. "Mr. Mariluch. Thank you for getting back to me." He listened for a moment, asked the man to hold, then cupped his hand around the phone. "You mind?"

She waved his question aside. "Not at all. I'll drive the twins. That way you won't feel rushed."

He grinned, mouthed *Thank you*, and returned to his call.

Luna skipped on ahead, her braids bouncing against her shoulders, while Callie hung back, shoulders slumped.

Evie took her hand and gave it a squeeze. "Let's go see about making this an amazing day. What do you say?"

"I guess."

"What's one thing you're looking forward to?"

She frowned, as if deep in thought, then smiled. "I know. When I get home, you, me, Daddy and Luna can give Aunt Martha our show. With the stage and curtains and everything."

"Sure. Although I meant during school."

"Oh. Recess, I guess."

Evie laughed. "That sounds fun."

As to their afternoon production, she wasn't sure how she felt about that. She had a feeling Monte would be more endearing than ever. Seeing his playful side made her wish she could stop time and delay her assignment indefinitely. But that was also why these interactions created substantial inner angst.

She knew the more attached she became to him and his girls, the deeper the ache would be once she left.

Monte was repairing a section of fence when Evie drove by in a swirl of dust. He felt an urge to drop what he was doing and jog after her. Instead, he reminded himself that he was a grown man and calmly, albeit quickly, finished.

Then hurried home.

As he passed the east pasture, his two ranch hands ribbed him, making it clear they knew precisely the reason for his rushed pace.

Inhaling, he raised his chin, squared his shoulders and slowed his feet.

This provided the added benefit of allowing his breathing to return to normal before reaching the house.

He followed the sound of Evie and his aunt's voice down the hall.

"I understand completely." Evie sounded concerned. "I just think the sooner you do so, the better."

He poked his head into his aunt's room. "The sooner you do what?"

Evie startled and both women looked at him with wide eyes.

He chuckled. "Didn't mean to scare you."

"We're fine." His aunt tidied up her bedside table. "Did you need something, dear?"

"Well, as long as you're asking… Any chance I can talk you into making some of your awesome strawberry-rhubarb pie?"

"Was already planning on it, along with a couple pans of brownies and two big ol' pots of chili."

"That sounds like too much work."

"It'll bring me joy, and you know it. And when the gals from church heard about your bull riding clinic, they insisted on bringing desserts. The Herrons plan on supplying some of their famous peach cobbler, and the girls from youth group are supposed to be bringing the fixings for a hot cocoa bar, too. Although the weatherman's predicting a beautiful day."

"I'd hate for them—"

Smiling, she held up a hand. "Before you say some rubbish about not wanting to put folks out—they insisted. It is the Sage Creek way, after all."

"True, and for that, I'm grateful." He told them about the call he'd received. "The guy sounds really interested, and he's looking to invest in more than one bull. But he wants to see some of the other boys perform. I invited him to come out this weekend."

Evie frowned. "But won't you be busy?"

"I told him that. He didn't seem to mind, so long as I planned on letting the guys ride, which I assured him I was. Besides, my 'wife' will be here." He grinned. As always, her blush only increased her beauty. "Figured Mr. Mariluch would be in good hands, considering what a great sales lady she was last time."

Aunt Martha frowned. "What're you talking about?"

Monte laughed and relayed how the man had referred to Evie the night of the rodeo.

"Hmm…" His aunt tapped her chin. "An interesting thought, for sure."

The pink in Evie's cheeks deepened, and she fiddled with an afghan on the chair that didn't need folding. She immediately excused herself to tackle household chores.

He tapped down a sudden urge to help.

He was in deep.

In no hurry to leave the house, he told his aunt more about his time at the rodeo. "We might have ourselves a superstar. The other bulls did well, too, but Jackhammer came out of the chutes ready for business."

"I'm glad. And based on that blush I saw on Evie's face a moment ago, and the way you both kept stealing glances at one another, I'm guessing the competition wasn't the only highlight."

"You're reading into things."

"I'm not and you know it. But I'll drop the subject so your face doesn't grow more flushed than it already is."

He turned toward the door before proving her statement true. "As entertaining as this conversation is, I've got work to do."

Her soft chuckle trailed him as he strode out of the room and down the hall. He stepped outside as Evie was climbing the porch steps.

"Hey." She paused with her hand on the railing. "I forgot to tell you, Callie asked if we could put on a show this afternoon."

"Bribery to get her to school?"

"Something like that."

"So long as you take the solo."

Her eyes widened. "What? As in singing?"

He laughed. "Just kidding."

She released a breath. "Thank goodness."

"Callie said she'd join you."

"Uh-huh. Right after your ballet intro, right?"

He tossed out a few other quips, reluctant to end their playful banter. But then his ranch hand pulled up in his pickup and shot him a knowing look that heated his face double what Aunt Martha's teasing had.

Travis parked and stepped out of his vehicle. He greeted Evie with a tip of his hat that revealed eyes hinting at laughter. "Ma'am."

She waved, said she had a date with a carrot, and sauntered off.

Travis watched her leave, then turned back to Monte. "Dude. Seems someone had a great weekend."

Monte rolled his eyes. "What are you, ten?"

"I saw the sparks flying between you two. It's about time, too. Because, let's face it, you're not getting any younger."

"You, my friend, are regressing by the minute." The best way to get the guy to leave him alone? Throw him a task. "How about you quit flapping your jaw and make yourself useful? I need you to help me feed these boys." He supplemented the bulls' diets with a high-protein grain. "Then we need to move them to the east pasture before they eat the grass to the ground and we end up with a mud pit come the next hard rain."

"What? This subject hitting too close to home?"

Shaking his head, Monte headed toward the barn where he stored the feed.

He spent the next few hours battling to keep his mind focused on the upcoming clinic, rather than the afternoon he'd spend with Evie and his girls. Their time together always felt so natural.

Would she say the same? Had she thought more about his request that she stay?

Could tonight help tip her decision in his favor?

Every day she remained meant more opportunities to capture her heart. He couldn't remember the last time he'd thought this way regarding a woman.

Actually, he could—his ex. He'd chased after her plenty, before she finally gave him a chance. Look how that had ended. Except Evie was as different to her as ranching was to high-rise living.

She was also accustomed to a world he knew little about.

With a sigh, he reviewed his pre-event checklist on his notes app. Although he was making good progress, he still had to take care of numerous details. Next up? Ensuring he had enough training equipment to accommodate the fifteen or so guys Declan had rallied together.

He phoned a buddy that worked at the local gym. He made small talk, asking about the guy's business and family, before explaining the reason for his call. "Any chance I can rent your medicine balls? Got some balance drills I want to run the riders through."

"Sure. How many?"

"How many can you spare?"

"Got two twelve-pounders, one fifteen, and one twenty."

Four total. Adding his and the three he was borrowing from friends meant he could accommodate nearly half his students. "That'll work." He'd put the men through a rotation.

He'd just finished locating a handful of fifty-five-gallon drums to convert into practice bucking barrels when the hum of Evie's car drew his attention.

Deciding to take a brief break, he strolled back to the house. From the looks of things, everyone—Callie included—was in a great mood.

Not surprising, considering she'd probably spent much of her day imagining how they'd perform the best show possible for Aunt Martha. That child was as creative as she was mischievous.

"Daddy!" Callie jumped into his arms.

Noting Evie's immediate grin, and feeling one come on himself, he gave his daughter a squeeze, deposited her back on her feet, and did the same with Luna. "You two have a good day?"

Callie nodded, eyes bright. "Ms. Vargas gave me fidget toys to play with and lets me stand up during reading if I want, so long as I go to the back and don't distract the other kids. Plus, she let me clean the white board and help hand out papers and stuff."

In other words, she found ways to allow for movement. Smart. And kind.

He looked at Evie, even more struck by her beauty now than when she'd first arrived, because now he knew the heart beneath her appearance. That made her radiant—and well worth holding on to.

After Luna shared the highlights of her day, they transitioned to discussing the show they planned to perform for his aunt. The girls had brainstormed quite an act.

Callie skipped ahead to the porch steps then stopped and turned around. "Can we practice now?"

He glanced at Evie.

She smiled, although she appeared a tad shy. Then again, the situation would probably feel awkward for them both, especially with Callie directing.

But they'd promised.

He rustled Callie's hair. "Fine with me."

When Evie gave a similar answer, both girls cheered and barreled inside, likely to rummage through their dress-up clothes for all manner of silly attire.

"This'll be interesting." He held the door open for Evie. "I appreciate your willingness to participate."

"I wouldn't miss it for the world."

The warmth in her expression suggested she was growing as fond of him and the twins as they were of her.

Maybe even fond enough to see herself becoming part of their lives for good.

Chapter Fourteen

Three encores and escalating shenanigans from the girls later, Evie found herself laughing so hard she developed a side ache. Thanks to her role as the "galloping reindeer," she was also feeling every bite of the supper they'd eaten prior.

Monte appeared equally amused. But he also seemed a bit protective of his aunt and, after a quick glance in her direction, suggested the theater call it a night.

The girls groaned, and Callie flopped onto the floor with enough melodrama to make Bette Davis proud.

"That's boring," she said.

"Come sit by me." Martha patted the couch cushions next to her. "How about we watch a movie?"

Pretty Polly Prankster?"

"Yes!" Luna plopped down on the other side of her aunt.

"I'll make popcorn." Monte darted into the kitchen and soon returned with a large bowl wafting buttery steam. Standing in the center of the living room, he eyed the open spot on the love seat next to Evie. He looked at Callie, now spread on her belly, occupying the second half of the couch. Was he debating asking the child to move over?

Seemed an easy enough request, unless he actually *wanted* to sit by Evie.

Her face heated, and her flutters extended beyond her stomach to her spine. She felt similar to how she had the day Mark Pitts had asked her to prom.

But despite her jitters, she also felt a sense of rightness when the cowboy sat beside her.

Wisdom, anchored in the reality that she wouldn't remain in Sage Creek long, encouraged her to keep her emotions in check. Yet, here she was, contemplating the question Monte had asked on their drive home from the rodeo. Common sense told her he wanted a stable caregiver for his aunt and the girls. But the way he'd been looking at her lately suggested his invitation went deeper.

If so, would she consider putting down roots in Sage Creek? And not just for him, as tempting as that was.

Could she actually be happy here? She knew from watching her parents and friends that marriage wasn't always silly fun and romantic evenings. Sometimes things got tough, especially on a ranch.

Then again, she'd encounter plenty of storms, regardless. Her mom and dad had also shown her that while loving someone didn't mean a problem-free life, it did mean not having to weather the rain alone.

There was no one she'd rather get drenched with than Monte.

As if he could read her thoughts, he slipped his hand under hers and interlocked their fingers.

She startled, her gaze shooting to his, any jitters she felt soothed by the warmth pouring from his eyes.

He leaned toward her, close enough that she could feel the heat radiating from him. "Something on your mind, Evie?" He kept his voice low.

Why did the way he spoke her name make her want to melt against him? "Just caught up in the storyline, I guess." The one she'd been fantasizing about between the two of them.

"Taking notes from these animated jokesters regarding what kind of mischief y'all may get into later?"

"Ha. Seems to me you fit that role better than I do."

"Hey, now, I resemble that remark." He laughed, then sobered. "Want to step outside for some fresh air?"

Yes! But she quickly tamped down her enthusiasm with a slow breath.

"Um…" She glanced at Aunt Martha, who, thankfully, either hadn't heard his question or didn't think anything of it. Then again, it was a bit warm in here, although she doubted that had anything to do with room temperature. "Sure." She stood and, with her hand still securely held in his, accompanied him onto the porch.

A cool breeze swept over her, and she shivered.

"Hold up." He dashed inside and returned with a throw blanket, which he wrapped around her shoulders.

He motioned to the bench swing, then sat beside her. "I appreciate what you did for Callie today. With her teacher. And that you helped me see that she needed help."

"Of course."

"When you first came, you mentioned you didn't have much experience with kids. You could've fooled me. I don't think I've ever seen Luna warm up to someone so quickly."

"She's precious. They both are."

"Pretty sure they think you're awesome as well. And I agree. The way you got Aunt Martha laughing…"

"As if your silly voices and accents didn't play a part in that?" She playfully bumped her shoulder against his.

"I knew my middle school days would prepare me for something. Seriously, though. I can't believe how well she's feeling. Whatever you're doing, keep it up."

She frowned and looked at her hands. Martha still hadn't told him. The longer she waited, the higher his hopes would rise. That would also give them much farther to crash.

"Hey." He gave her hand a squeeze. "Did I say something wrong?"

If only she could tell him. It wasn't like he or his aunt would file charges or even report to her boss that she'd broken confidentiality. But that wouldn't make sharing Martha's decision with Monte right. No matter how much she wished otherwise.

Yet, her silence was the only thing keeping her here. Was that influencing her behavior?

No. She'd signed an oath, and while the Bowmans might not disclose her actions, God would know. She chose to trust that if she followed His ways, He'd take care of everything else—even if that meant losing the best man she'd ever met.

Sensing Monte waiting for an answer, she shook her head. "Just thinking."

"About?"

"Lazy evenings and how beautiful it is here." That was true enough, as the thought entered her mind the moment she gazed at the star-dotted sky.

"I'm glad to hear that. Your company called today to verify that our needs hadn't changed before sending out your replacement. I asked them if it was possible for you to stay."

She sucked in a breath.

"Not that you have to, or even that I expect you to. I just wanted to know where things stood, contractually."

"And?"

"The gal said she didn't have authority to speak to that but that she'd relay my question to those who did. You may receive a phone call in the next day or two."

"Okay." Most likely, her company would love his idea. They wouldn't want to replace a caregiver a client trusted with someone with whom he might not click.

What if his aunt never gained the courage to explain her choice? Granted, she wouldn't be able to keep that hidden forever. Eventually, her condition would reveal itself. Although she could leave him to assume the chemo hadn't worked. Most people wouldn't even question that, based on the prognosis of recurrent ovarian cancer.

But Evie would know. Could she live with that, were they to develop a relationship? Or would she feel haunted that she'd willingly, maybe even for decades, kept such a devastating secret from the man she loved?

She was overthinking things. The guy had asked her to extend her assignment, not pledge her life to him. Yet, she couldn't stop entertaining the possibility—along with all the what-ifs accompanying the scenario.

"Something wrong?" He regarded her with a furrowed brow.

She swallowed and shook her head. "Just processing."

"Anything related to what I asked on our drive back from Dripping Springs?"

"About a lot of things." She felt like a tangled mess of hope, sorrow, guilt and anxiety.

He smoothed a breeze-stirred lock of hair from her face, his thumb tracing the contour of her cheek. "Think you can handle hanging around a bit longer?"

She opened her mouth to respond, but he pressed his index finger to her lips. "Just give it some prayer."

"I can do that." His statement reminded her of all the times she'd told God of her longing to find someone with whom she could envision spending the rest of her life. She couldn't imagine a better, more loyal man than Monte to unite her life with, and she adored those girls. Martha, too.

As astounding as it was, considering her impression when she first arrived—she felt like she belonged here. With him.

Lord, please give Martha the strength to be honest with her nephew, preferably before he starts planning her remission celebration. And don't let him hate me when she does tell him.

Monte breathed in the clear night air, Evie's soft floral scent drawing him to her. He could tell his request left her conflicted. He liked to think that meant she too was considering where God might take them.

He'd be wise not to push her, regardless how "urgent" the issue felt.

His gut told him God had brought her here for more than Aunt Martha's care. He needed to trust his Father would work everything out, if not before her replacement came, then after somehow. As numerous Bible stories so clearly demonstrated, again and again, seemingly impossible situations merely served as backdrops to display God's power.

He sure could use divine help, because he had no intention of losing the most beautiful woman, inside and out, he'd ever met.

The fact that they could sit, content to gaze up at the stars without feeling the need to fill the moment with mindless chatter counted for something.

The creaking of the swing merged with the occasional call of a great horned owl. The nearly full moon cast the land in a silvery glow, reminding him of why he'd never want to live anywhere else.

He hoped Evie was beginning to feel the same.

Watching for her reaction, he held his breath, placed his arm around her and gently nudged her closer. She tensed, then exhaled and leaned back against his chest. Arms around her waist, hands interlocked at her belly and her strawberry-scented hair tickling his face, he closed his eyes and prayed for many evenings just like this.

Evie's breathing slowed and deepened. She remained so still, he wondered if she'd fallen asleep. The thought increased his reluctance for their time together to end.

But then she sat up straight.

"We should probably get inside." She stood.

"Right." He'd been selfish to leave Aunt Martha to watch over the girls for this long, especially since she tended to get so fatigued by day's end. This was probably doubly true now, after all this evening's activity, her belly laughs included.

He dashed to the door to open it for Evie, then followed her inside. They entered as the credits started to play on the twins' movie.

Callie sprang to her feet. "Beauty parlor time!"

Monte crossed his arms. The child was well practiced in coming up with reasons to delay her bedtime. "It's a little late for that."

His aunt smiled. "Tomorrow. That'll give me time to run in town for those fancy nail stickers you girls love so much. An early Christmas gift."

Callie groaned but complied, and soon was chattering on about what colors and designs she'd choose and how she wanted her hair done. By the time they left for school the next morning, Luna had caught her enthusiasm, and they were both planning yet another show—this one fashion.

Midmorning, Evie called him to tell him she was running into town to purchase dress-up clothes from the local thrift store.

He met her at her car when she returned, his heart swelling at the obvious joy radiating from her face, and not just because she was gorgeous. It was the cause of her joy that most deeply touched him. She was excited to surprise the girls.

Because she loved them.

Grinning, she stepped out of her vehicle. "Wait until you see what I found." She retrieved two full bags from the back seat and began pulling dresses out one by one and draping them over her shoulder.

The first was a red gown that would be the perfect length for the twins. The second was satiny blue with an intricate lace design over the skirt, and another was decorated with beading and gold embossed flowers.

He chuckled. "They'll love them. How much do I owe you?"

"Nothing. When the store owner learned who I was and why I was buying all this, she refused to charge me. Said your aunt has done more for her and her family over the years than she could ever repay."

A lump lodged in his throat at the reminder of yet another life his aunt had touched, and how this community always cared for their own. "Wow."

"That's what I said. Sage Creek has some of the kindest, most thoughtful people I've ever encountered."

"Best place to live, hands down."

If she sensed his hidden message, she didn't let on.

She glanced at her phone screen. "That time already?" She returned her purchases to the bag. "I best go pick up the girls."

She dashed into the house and returned empty-handed.

"Mind if I join you?"

"Not at all."

The way she smiled back at him made him think she welcomed the idea.

He took her hand, her skin soft and warm against his. "How about we take my truck?"

She turned to him with a furrowed brow, her eyes searching his.

He held his breath, mentally preparing himself for the sting of rejection.

But then her posture relaxed and, with her fingers intertwined with his, she resumed walking.

This time he couldn't hold back his grin—at least, not until he glanced toward the arena and he caught Travis watching him with a teasing smirk.

He frowned, but refused to release Evie's hand. He was starting to believe she might stay, which meant he might as well get used to Travis's ribbing.

They talked comfortably on the drive to the school, mainly about the upcoming clinic. Evie seemed to be looking forward to the event, as if she felt personally invested.

He'd never felt that with Erin. Although she'd acted supportive, her enthusiasm had always felt off. Evie was different. She seemed to care, not just about what mattered to him, but about him as a person.

As if she were happy and content to be in his presence, whether that meant sitting around the breakfast table or driving into town to pick up the twins.

At the school, he and Evie went in to get the girls together. While he hadn't had the best relationship experience prior, his heart told him this was what true love felt like.

As expected, the girls hadn't forgotten about the "beauty parlor" activity. Although they wanted to hurry home and start first thing, he told them they'd need to finish homework first.

"You mind helping the girls on your own this afternoon?" he asked Evie. "I need to catch up on some things." One thing he knew for sure, he wanted to be around when she showed the girls their dresses.

"Got it covered."

"Maybe hold off on the rest until I get back?"

"Absolutely."

He didn't know what he was looking forward to most—watching them light up when they saw all the bling, or catching Evie's reaction once they did. The fact that he'd get to do both made him work extra hard and triple fast.

An hour and a half later, he arrived home out of breath and feeling more sentimental than he'd expected at the thought of Evie dolling up his girls. Like he'd seen countless moms do with their daughters in various social media reels.

He'd not realized how much he longed for the twins to experience the same thing until this very moment.

"Hey, there." Evie emerged from the kitchen holding a toy rolling pin. "The girls and I just finished making playdough cookies."

Luna approached him holding out a plate of purple-and-green-splotched circles. "You hungry, Daddy?"

"Starved." He shot Evie a wink, delighted by the blush this triggered. "Where's Aunt Martha?"

"Visiting the horses."

He blinked. "Really?"

Her gaze faltered. "She hasn't been out long."

Was she worried he'd be upset she'd allowed his aunt to venture off without her? "That's great." With how cheerful his aunt had been lately, he wasn't about to tell Evie how to do her job.

"I'll go get her now." She handed Callie the rolling pin. "Seeing how the beauty parlor's about to open."

"Yay!" Both girls began jumping in place.

He was surprised to see Callie so enthused for such a "girly-girl" endeavor. Then again, she *did* love anything with a dramatic element, and, it seemed, that involved Evie.

He could relate.

Their excitement multiplied once Evie returned and showed them her thrift store finds. She'd also purchased scented lotions. Declaring the salon open, she treated them all, Aunt Martha included, to a manicure.

"Can we play rockstar now?" Callie asked.

Evie frowned. "Rain check? I need to catch up on the laundry. I promised your sister I'd wash her favorite dress for tomorrow."

The twins looked so dejected, he couldn't help but laugh. "You relax." He waved a hand. "I know how to run clothes through the machine."

"You sure?"

"It'll give me something productive to do while I make some phone calls."

She thanked him, and he strolled down the hall to the sound of the girls' cheers erupting once again.

He carted all three hampers, one at a time, into the mudroom, and dumped their contents into the large industrial sink for sorting. Not surprisingly, almost all of Callie's new clothes were smudged with dirt and grass stains. Equally predictable, none of Luna's were. He could easily envision her and her friends daintily swinging while her sister found a hill to tumble down or sandbox to dig through.

With room for a few more colored items, he grabbed a pair of his aunt's pants. A crinkling sound reminded him to empty her pockets. In one, he found a wrapped piece of ginger candy, tissue and a few coins. In the other, he found two receipts. He was about to throw them into the trash when two words—San Marcos—caught his eye. He read the receipt more carefully, noting the date and time.

Odd, and certainly not anywhere his aunt would've been recently, especially not midmorning last Thursday. She'd probably picked up someone's litter.

After tossing a few more items into the machine, he added detergent and adjusted the settings. With one load washing, he grabbed the empty hampers and strolled back down the hall, whistling a tune to a commercial that had popped into his mind.

As he neared the living room, the sound of his aunt's laughter stopped him midstep.

She'd been in high spirits lately—ever since the doctor came out to check her blood and ended up canceling that week's appointment. He'd expected her to feel as bummed with the delay as he'd been. When she hadn't appeared so, he thought she'd been trying to remain positive for his sake.

But she'd also told him she was done fighting. Never knowing her to give up easily, he'd assumed her comments had stemmed from momentary fatigue she'd soon overcome.

What if she'd been serious?

No. Evie would've told him.

His gut felt hollow as he stood, watching her paint Callie's toenails.

His aunt glanced up, worry lines immediately stretching across her forehead. "Monte, what's wrong? Has something happened?"

He stepped deeper into the room. "I never asked. How'd your treatment go this past Thursday?"

She and Evie exchanged a look of guilt if ever he saw one before his aunt covered with a tight smile. "We've all heard the saying, 'Hurry up and wait.'" Her chuckle sounded forced. "You know how it is."

"Actually, I don't. How about you tell me?"

She picked up a sheet of stickers from the coffee table and studied it as if it contained the most fascinating designs she'd ever seen. "It's a busy clinic, is all. With so many people coming and going, I bet the doctors barely get a moment to catch their breath."

"You saying they rushed you?"

"Oh, I've never felt that."

She was trying hard not to outright lie, but that didn't make her evasive responses any less deceptive.

Heat surged through him. "You never went, did you?" And the fact that she tried so hard to keep that from him proved she'd made a deliberate choice.

She startled at his raised tone. "Monte, please." Her voice quivered. "I told you I couldn't do it anymore. You have to understand."

"Understand what? That you're giving up because this is hard?" Her tears pierced his heart, but he wouldn't allow emotions—not hers, his, or anyone else's for that matter—dictate such an important decision. "The girls and I need you." He shook his head. "I'm not letting you give up on yourself. Or on them."

Her shoulders trembled as she covered her face with her hands, her crying turning to deep-chested sobs.

He hurried to her and rubbed her back. "I shouldn't have

gotten so upset. I recognize how difficult this has been, and I promise you that I'll walk beside you every step of the way. I won't leave you to face this battle alone. Now is not the time to declare defeat."

He turned to Evie. "How could you keep something like this from me?"

She was now standing, facing him. "She's my patient. I'm bound by confidentiality."

"Yeah, well, I'm technically your boss. As such, I'm telling you to call the clinic first thing tomorrow to get her treatments rescheduled. And see to it you get her there next time."

She took in a deep breath as if steeling herself. "I know this is painful to hear and even more so to accept, but this is her decision."

He scoffed. "Yeah, well. Then it's your job, as her paid caregiver, to change her mind."

"Actually, it's not." Her voice carried barely above a whisper.

He felt like he'd been whacked in the chest with an iron bar. "Then I guess your services are no longer needed."

Chapter Fifteen

That night, Evie tossed and turned, rehashing her conversation with Martha the day she'd revealed her bucket list. Should she have tried to talk her out of her decision? Her training said, ethically, that was the last thing she was supposed to do. Give detailed information and answer questions honestly, yes. Pressure someone with a potentially terminal illness into spending the last few years, if not fewer, of their lives sick from chemo?

No. She couldn't do that to Martha, regardless of how much she loved Monte.

And she did love him, which was why it hurt so badly knowing how much he hated her now. Eyeing her opened suitcase lying on the floor, she told herself she'd eventually heal and forget all about him and her time in Sage Creek. But she feared that would never happen. Nor would she ever encounter another man like Monte Bowman—of that she was certain.

Feeling as if her heart were tearing in two, she cried herself asleep and awoke with bloodshot and puffy eyes. She emerged downstairs to find Martha's door closed, the girls watching cartoons in the living room, and Monte making coffee in the kitchen.

He turned toward her as she entered. His expression would've implied lack of emotion, if not for the pain in his eyes. "Morning."

"Morning." She should've known he had too much integrity to give her the silent treatment. "Monte?"

He almost seemed to wince at her mention of his name.

"I wanted to tell you."

"I don't want to talk about this now."

"I know you'd like me to leave, but I also know you were expecting me here, able to help, when you scheduled your clinic. I'd like to stay through that, if you'll let me."

He released a breath and rubbed a hand over his face. Then nodded. "I appreciate that."

For the next few days, their conversations remained equally short. When the girls asked why their father wasn't around for meals, Evie said he was busy preparing for his upcoming event. While true, she also feared he was avoiding her.

She woke early the morning of his clinic to find him in the kitchen and the rest of the house asleep.

She poured herself a cup of coffee and lingered near the table before sitting across from him. "I've been praying for this weekend."

He glanced up from the notebook pages from which he'd been working, and for a moment, she saw a hint of his affection toward her. But then his expression deadpanned. "Thanks."

Lord, give me the words that will help him understand.

Yet, she knew he did, and that he wasn't truly angry at her. He was grieving the woman who had been there for him and the twins when they needed her most. The one who, up until recently, had in many ways held the family together.

Unrealistic or not, Monte had hung all his hopes on Evie.

She wrapped her hands around her mug. "What time will people start arriving?"

"Eight. I'll set up a folding table in front of the porch. I printed off a bunch of liability forms for people to sign. Minors need a signature from a parent or guardian."

"Okay. I heard a storm may come through."

He gave one firm nod. "Hoping it'll hold off until tomorrow night. If not, we'll have to cut things short. And reimburse folks."

"I'm sorry."

He shrugged. "Can't have them, or my bulls, slopping around in the mud. Nor am I willing to tear up the arena. Until then, we'll pretend like the forecast predicted nothing but rainbows and sunshine."

Had they had this conversation a few days ago, she might've made a teasing comment regarding how rainbows formed.

He pushed back from the table and stood. "I'm about to run into town to pick up ice and whatnot. Mind cleaning out the girls' wading pool? I'd like to use it to keep drinks cold."

"Of course."

He held her gaze. "I appreciate your help."

Tears pricked her eyes at the grief in his—and on a day he should feel excitement. Then again, that was what made cancer so difficult. It tended to taint everything gray. "It's the least I can do."

By the time Martha meandered into the kitchen, he'd already left. "I'm sorry about what happened the other night. I meant to tell him. I just didn't know how to get the words out."

"I understand."

"He'll come to as well. Just give him time."

She nodded, but they both knew she didn't have that. She'd finally met a man that she could envision spending the rest of her life with, and it had to be here, and now? When she knew the only possible outcome would be her leaving with a shattered heart?

The twins didn't emerge until nearly nine. They stepped outside fed, dressed, and with their hair brushed—verifying what Monte had said the night he learned about Martha's decision.

They didn't need her anymore.

Evie was already sitting behind a card table, handling check-ins. She flashed the twins a smile. "Morning." A handful of eager cowboys were lined up in front of her and more still gathered outside the arena.

"Can we help?" Callie hovered at her side, Luna half a step behind her. Still in their pajamas, they had to be cold.

"Once you get some warm clothes on, absolutely." Turning back to the man filling out a form before her, she excused herself and returned with two of the rockers from the porch.

The girls returned wearing boots and jackets and looking as proud as the evening they'd gone mutton busting.

And Evie had admitted to herself how she felt about Monte.

Averting her thoughts before the pain swelling within left her undone, she spent the rest of the morning alternating between keeping the girls entertained and acting as event director so Monte could focus on attendees.

About an hour before lunch, half a dozen ladies from the church arrived, all bearing a dish. They set these out, along with the massive pots of chili Martha had made. Not long after, a couple who owned a local peach orchard came bearing large pans of still-steaming cobbler.

Setting out napkins and paper plates, Evie surveyed it all. "Wow. You all are amazing."

One of Martha's friends smiled. "We're happy to do it. The Bowmans have always been the first to help a person in need. And after all Monte has done for sweet Martha..." She gazed toward the arena. "It's nice to see the good Lord bless him in this way. Matter of fact, we can cover things from here."

"I appreciate the offer, but I'm okay."

"I'm sure you are. But the girls are liable to get bored hanging around here soon enough, and everyone knows how Callie behaves when that happens."

She laughed. "I'll take her and Luna to their tree house shortly."

"May want to hurry. Despite how the sky looks now, if things don't shift, we're in for rain."

"Hopefully it'll hold off until after Monte's event." He didn't need disappointment added to his grief.

"Ms. Evie, watch what I can do."

She turned around to see Callie, arms outstretched, using the porch railing like it was a balance beam.

"Down please." While a fall from that height wouldn't be life-threatening, it could result in an injury.

Callie groaned and made no move to comply.

Evie narrowed her eyes. "I mean it."

"Fine." She jumped off, landing frog-like in the gravel. "But there's nothing to do."

Evie relayed where she planned to take her and her sister.

"Yeah! Come on!" Callie grabbed Luna by the hand and they raced off, with both dogs following close behind.

The guy who'd brought the cobbler chuckled. "That's one way to keep that child out of trouble."

"That's the plan."

Although she needed to hurry and catch up with her. Experience verified it wouldn't take long for the girl to create mischief.

Out of breath, she reached them at their tree house. Luna was in the tire swing while Callie was pushing with all the strength her forty-some-pound frame could muster.

"Hop on and I'll push you both."

This occupied them long enough for Evie's arms to grow tired. She was about to tell the twins she'd ran out of oomph, when they decided to "go to their fort"—an alcove in the trees they'd turned into a secret hideout.

"Girls only," Callie said. "Except for Daddy. But he needs a ticket."

Evie tried to mirror the child's serious expression. "I see. And how much does that cost?"

The girls looked at one another with furrowed brows.

"A dollar?" Callie asked her sister.

"Or ice cream." Luna grinned.

"With marshmallows and chocolate syrup. The kind that gets hard once you pour it on."

Evie laughed. "What'll you charge me?"

The girls once again exchanged a quizzical expression, but then, Luna said, "Nothing. Cuz you're our friend."

Callie nodded. "And a girl."

Tears pricked her eyes to think of the relationship God had helped them build in such a short time. When she'd arrived on the ranch, she'd prayed for the ability to earn their trust. She'd never anticipated how attached the twins would become to her, or her to them.

To Monte, as well. In fact, she'd spent a great deal of will-power trying not to fall for the man. Until the day she'd stopped fighting her emotions and let herself dream of what they might become.

This would be her hardest goodbye yet.

Taking a deep breath, she swallowed down the wave of sorrow threatening to overtake her and sat upon a sun-warmed rock while the girls pranced to and from their fort playing pioneer. The dogs followed, sniffing about as if engaged in a highly serious mission.

Inhaling the soothing scent of decomposing wood and damp earth, Evie removed her shoes and socks and immersed her feet in the cool creek water. She reflected upon her mental quip, upon first arriving, that this assignment would be far from a spa experience.

Her prediction had been right. This—breathing the fresh air, listening to the birds chirping and the girls laughing, golden rays filtering through the trees—was far better. A soul-deep sanctuary she'd never experienced in the city.

A shadow fell upon her as windswept clouds engulfed the

sun. A droplet landed on her head, then on her shoulder, then another.

She surveyed the sky, noting the thick blanket of gray advancing toward them. "Girls, it's time to head back."

They groaned.

"Five more minutes?" Callie was squatting beneath an umbrella of trees, picking at a fallen and decaying branch patched with sage-toned lichen.

Shaking her head, Evie put her socks and shoes back on. "It's about to rain."

"We don't care."

She studied the sky again. Those clouds looked ominous.

She stood. "How about if we get some of that peach cobbler Aunt Martha's friends brought over?"

Although clearly disappointed, Luna complied. Callie, however, darted back into the woods. "Come find me!"

Evie made eye contact with Luna. "Wait here, please." She hurried after her sister. "Now is not the time for hide-and-seek." As she stepped beneath a canopy of enmeshed branches, bushes and vines sprouting between them, the wind picked up and the sky unleashed an icy onslaught.

Thunder boomed.

Evie shivered as rain slicked her clothes to her skin. "Callie, I mean it. One. Two."

Branches rustled, and a moment later, the child reemerged, drenched, muddy, shivering, and with twigs tangled in her hair.

"Come on." She reached for the child's hand and tugged her back toward the creek.

She turned at a yelp and a yank on her arm to find Callie sitting on the ground, holding her ankle, clearly fighting tears.

Evie rushed toward her and squatted to eye level. "Sweetie, are you okay?" It appeared she'd stumbled into a cavity formed between a jumble of thick, exposed roots.

"It hurts."

Max sniffed at the child's face, then licked her cheek. She pushed him away.

"Can you walk on it?"

She tried to stand, then winced.

Lightning lit the sky, and the wind moaned through the leaves. Behind them, Luna called out for her, frightened, and likely near frozen.

A surge of adrenaline shot through Evie. "We're coming."

Callie wasn't heavy by any means, but neither was Evie all that strong. Yet, she needed to figure out something, or it'd take forever for them to find shelter.

She turned so that her back faced the child and patted her shoulders. "Hop on."

With icy arms wrapped around her neck and legs around her waist, she rose with a grunt, her thighs burning beneath the strain. Rain pelting her face, she hustled back to the creek to find Luna sitting on the rock, lips slightly blue.

By now, the sky held a dark, greenish tint, and the gravel road leading to the house felt impossibly long. Passing the stables, she briefly contemplated seeking cover among the horses.

Did tornadoes ever hit the hill country in mid-December? They needed to find shelter, quickly, just in case. But she assumed the thin wooden walls could be more dangerous than protective.

Plus, what if Monte freaked out and came looking for them? That would put him at risk as well.

As if on cue, a muscular form resembling their dad raced toward them. He met them drenched and with piercing, determined eyes.

He looked at Callie and the crevice between his brows deepened. "She hurt?"

Fighting to keep her voice steady despite her mounting fear, Evie told him what had happened.

"Give her to me." He lifted his daughter off Evie's back

with the ease of someone carrying a down-filled pillow. "Y'all run on ahead."

She frowned, fear for him and the other child making her reluctant to leave.

But his directive made sense. The best way she could help was to get Luna inside and hunkered down in a back closet. That was why, when he repeated the command, with more force this time, she nodded, took Luna's cold hand in hers and jogged off as fast as the girl could keep up.

Martha was waiting for them on the porch, soaked, and looking even more terrified than Evie felt, if that were possible. "Monte and Callie?"

Evie explained, ushering the woman back inside. "They'll be here shortly." She scanned their surroundings for a secure area far from windows. The pantry was too small for all of them. The twin's closet would be better. She urged Martha and Luna deeper into the house. Remembering her emergency preparedness training, she dashed into the kitchen for a pitcher of sweet tea—the quickest and easiest liquid to grab.

With every second feeling like a hundred, she prayed that, if a tornado was indeed coming, God would hold back the storm until Monte and Callie arrived.

Monte burst into the house as a living room window shattered, and the howling wind and battering hail grew louder. Callie shrieked, tightened her grip and buried her face into his chest, as if his body could shield her from the storm.

If necessary, it would. He'd cover her faster than it took lightning to flash. But he'd much rather get her someplace more secure—and check on the others.

Thank goodness he'd had enough common sense to send everyone from the workshop home once the sky started darkening.

Running down the hall, he called out to them. If they replied, he couldn't hear them above the storm. At least they'd all made it inside. He hated to think what might've happened if Evie hadn't responded as quickly as she had. Or if he hadn't found them in time to carry Callie back.

All three of them could've been whacked and buried by falling branches.

The thought nauseated him.

Had he been thinking straight, he would've taken the ATV.

He tore into the twins' bedroom, pulse pounding in his ears, lunged for the closet and threw open the door. Relief nearly buckled his knees. Aunt Martha, Evie and Luna were all huddled together under the child's favorite velvety blanket. Head resting against Evie, his daughter clutched her stuffed elephant under her chin.

They all scooched over, and he deposited a shivering Callie next to Evie on her other side. She wrapped an arm around the child's shoulder, held her close and began to sing. A trained ear might call her off-key and unmelodious. Yet, he wasn't sure he'd ever heard—or seen—anything more beautiful.

Chapter Sixteen

The wind died down as quickly as it arrived. Monte released a breath, not knowing what state he'd find the house in but more grateful than he could express that God had kept the four people he most cared about safe.

He tried anyway—thanking His Father while asking for help in making sense of the confusing thoughts the storm had evoked. He'd known, when he told Evie she needed to leave, that he'd be devastated once she did. When the storm hit, he'd realized he might actually lose her, and not just to a relocation. He'd felt like he was about to lose everything that made life worth living.

That included Evie.

But she'd come to do a job and had failed—for lack of trying. Then kept that from him. Maybe she thought he would grieve and move on, but what about the girls? Seemed to him, if she really loved them as much as she seemed to, she would've found a way to talk his aunt out of giving up.

While he wasn't thrilled with his aunt's decision, he could at least understand it. She was tired and discouraged. Evie should've expected that. When she'd arrived, he'd stressed the importance of acting as his aunt's cheerleader.

Instead, she'd defended his aunt's choice.

How could he let that go?

He stood on legs cramped from a burst of adrenaline followed by confinement in a small space. "Y'all stay here while I check things out."

They nodded, and he left to survey the damage. Everything remained untouched except the living room, where a thick branch protruded through the window, and glass shards and a splattering of hail spread across the carpet. The Christmas tree had fallen against the wall, but it was intact and the handful of presents beneath it seemed okay.

Outside, the hail had dented the vehicles and left ice balls nearly the size of a quarter. A section of the shed had ripped off, and a couple trees were down, one of them uprooted.

Looked like they'd be having another bonfire soon.

Heaviness weighted his chest as he thought back to their last one—the four of them, Evie included, gathered under the stars. Her being there had felt so right. Like she'd belonged.

He'd trusted her. Believed in her. One of the gals in his Bible study class had even declared her an answer to prayer.

Seemed to him, if that were true, his aunt wouldn't be surrendering to a terminal disease.

She's not. She's coming home.

The thought, soft but clear, hit him with such force, his gut said it came from God.

Jaw clenched, he shook his head. *I can't believe that. I won't.*

He'd never been one to argue with the Father. But neither was he ready to attribute divine origin to a whisper that drifted through his mind.

Because he wasn't certain or didn't want to hear it?

With a sigh, he resumed his brief inspection of his property. He suspected the dogs had hunkered down in the stable, and the cattle within eyesight seemed okay. He'd check them more carefully for injuries later.

Thankfully, it would take a mighty strong wind to toss about fifteen hundred pounds of muscle.

The dogs trotted out of the barn, looking a little disoriented but unharmed.

Relieved, he turned back to the house to clean up the glass in the living room.

He found Evie already doing that as the twins' boisterous voices drifted toward them.

She stood as he entered. "How extensive is the damage?"

"Not bad." He joined her near the busted window and squatted down to help.

"I've got this. I'm sure you have plenty to deal with outside."

True. He also needed to call his insurance agent. "I appreciate it."

He rose and was heading back out when his aunt's voice stopped him, asking him to wait for her.

When she met him at the door, he regarded her with a frown. "You're not planning to help me haul debris, are you?"

With a quick glance behind her, she shook her head and nudged him onto the porch. "Wanted to talk with you a minute."

He nodded. He wanted to think the storm had the girls asking questions she wanted him to prepare for—like were the dogs and horses okay or what happened to squirrels and such. But after all that had occurred, he feared the conversation would land much heavier than that.

Aunt Martha motioned toward the rocking chairs. He complied.

She sat as well and folded her hands in her lap. Her delay intensified his concern.

"I know how painful things have been—and still are." Her eyes searched his with a tenderness and compassion that clamped his heart in a vise. "I never meant to hurt you. I was trying so hard not to, wanting to find the right words and time to tell you what I knew you'd been praying against."

Guilt churned his gut. She was the one dying, yet she was comforting him. That had always been her way. As much as he longed to change her mind, he wouldn't make this conversation harder for her.

She'd suffered enough.

She took his hand in hers. "Sweetie, I didn't make this decision lightly."

"I know." She'd probably spent many sleepless nights and anxious days fretting and praying over it—and all on her own. "I wish we could've talked through this together."

"I'm sorry."

He shook his head. "No, I mean, I wish I hadn't been so bullheaded, so that you wouldn't have had to stress about how I would respond."

She offered a gentle smile. "You've always loved fiercely."

"Must be hereditary." He released a heavy breath, fighting to suppress the grief that otherwise could overwhelm him. Wanting to show his aunt the same strength she was displaying now.

After all she'd given to this family, and all she'd endured, it was the least he could do.

He rubbed at his thumb knuckle. "What now?"

"Not sure. I'll call the doctor tomorrow. But I suspect you and the girls will have to put up with me for a little while longer." She gave his arm a playful slap. "Then, we'll have hospice come in."

The word squeezed the air from his lungs. Fortifying himself against the threat of tears, he nodded. "I'll make sure you have the best care possible."

She paused. "Speaking of…"

He shook his head. "I know what you're about to say, but I can't."

"She didn't betray you, nor did she do anything wrong. To the contrary. She acted with the utmost integrity, even though doing so tore her up inside. You staying mad at her won't keep me around any longer than the good Lord allows. But it will drive away the gift He deposited on your doorstep."

"I'm not upset with her. Not anymore." Truly, he never had been. He'd merely blamed her for a situation he didn't want to accept. "I just don't think my heart can handle more loss."

"You mean when she leaves?"

He nodded.

"Then convince her to stay."

"You make it sound so easy."

"Oh, I think it will be. Matter of fact, I'm certain that sweet woman in there is waiting for you to give her reason to unpack that suitcase of hers for good."

A flicker of hope sparked within him. "Guess now I'm the one who'll be praying for the right words and timing."

"That's my boy." She stood. "How about you do that on your way into town for some window plastic before another storm blows through or a hefty rain turns our carpet and furniture soggy."

"I'll do that."

This was one discussion he didn't want to flub, especially after how he'd spoken to Evie a few nights prior, and how he'd treated her since.

What if she didn't want to hear anything he had to say?

Or if she listened, understood and rejected him anyway?

But what if Aunt Martha was right and God had brought Evie here, to this ranch, to give him a second chance at love?

Evie had just finished depositing a cardboard box of glass shards into the outside trash when Monte returned from his trip to the hardware store. A twinge of anxiety tempted her to hustle back inside, but she'd determined long ago not to allow fear of potential conflict dictate her actions.

Besides, there was no point in delaying the conversation.

Now that his event was over, cut short by the hail, he'd probably want her to leave immediately.

Then again, he might give her until first thing in the morning. That would lead to a strained and painful supper—if he joined them.

Swallowing a sigh, she waited for Monte at the bottom of the porch stairs. "Hey."

"Hey. Care to take a walk with me?"

"Sure." Her stomach felt queasy as she fell into step beside him. She glanced at the empty arena as they passed. "Sorry you weren't able to hold your full clinic."

He shrugged. "Managed to finish half of it. And I'll offer a makeup day to those who want it and reimburse the others. Several had already said they were hoping I'd host another event soon, and some talked about bringing their buddies along. Since I didn't spend much to put it on, it was almost all profit."

"That's great."

"Next time, I'll have to figure out how to feed everyone on the cheap. Otherwise, the stomachs in those guys could easily land me in debt."

"I wouldn't be surprised if your church family took care of the food again."

"Those gals do like to cook and bake, that's for sure. You try any of the Herrings' peach cobbler?"

"Not yet, but I plan to. They slipped a pan into the fridge for us. Said otherwise, they feared we might be too busy to snatch ourselves any before the cowboys demolished it." She asked if the man from the rodeo ever showed.

"Yep. Must've liked what he saw, because he walked away the proud sponsor of five of my derbies. Plus, I got four other investors and three strong maybes."

"Awesome!"

He nodded. "Seems the good Lord heard my prayers after all and plans to keep the ranch running a spell longer."

She frowned, knowing he wouldn't say the same in regard to his aunt.

If his words from the night he found out still conveyed his feelings, he blamed Evie.

Tears pricked her eyes. She blinked them away. "I'm really glad everything went so well."

"I had a lot of help."

"Your community is truly amazing."

"You think so?"

"Absolutely."

"Enough to consider sticking around?"

Her heart stuttered. Had he really asked what she thought he had?

She stopped and faced him, unsuccessfully trying to contain her hope. "What are you saying?"

"I'd like you to stay."

She wanted to as well, more than anything. Only not as a caregiver, although she realized Martha would need one. She also understood why Monte might feel reluctant to bring in someone new and unknown. And she felt a level of responsibility to accept his invitation.

But if she stayed, it had to be forever. Otherwise, she feared she'd never recover once she drove away.

Besides, with his aunt no longer receiving chemo, she wouldn't need help for a while. She told him this, as gently as possible, as they both recognized she meant once Martha went on hospice.

"Evie." Eyes locked onto hers, he took her hands in his. "I never should've lashed out at you like I did. You were doing your job, and you've been great. More than great." His Adam's apple bobbed down then up. "It's no surprise that you captured my aunt's and girls' hearts. What did surprise me, however, was how you seized mine."

The tears she'd been holding back slid down her cheek. "Oh, Monte."

He thumbed them away. "You are the most beautiful, caring, insightful, kind and compassionate woman I've ever met. I can't count how many times I've caught you looking at the girls with adoration in your eyes. Or making my aunt laugh, even if that meant acting like a galloping horseman." He quirked a teasing smile.

She crossed her arms in mock annoyance. "And whose idea was that?"

He chuckled. "Guilty. But you went along with it easily enough."

"It was fun."

"See what I mean? Entertaining, hilarious, creative."

"Did someone give you a thesaurus?" she teased.

"I'm just getting started. I have a list of accurate adjectives at the ready."

"Do you, now?"

"Yes, ma'am. And there's only one way to get this rambling cowboy to shut up."

"What's that?"

"Tell me you'll stay. Permanently." He pulled a small box wrapped in shiny red paper from his pocket.

"What's that?"

"An early Christmas gift."

"But I didn't get you anything." She'd meant to take the girls into town so they could pick out something together. But then the beauty parlor night had happened.

"There's only one gift I want this year." He motioned for her to open her present.

She complied, to reveal a velvet jewelry box. "When did you—?"

"Stopped in one of the boutiques—they've got a jewelry section in the back—before the hardware store." He dropped to one knee. "Evie Bell, will you marry me?"

She held out her hand, warmth spreading through her as he slipped a simple but gorgeous diamond ring on her finger. "Oh, Monte."

"Is that a yes?"

"I'm not going anywhere. Ever."

A grin erupted on his face, and his eyes widened. He stood, and his expression sobered as he cupped her face in his hands and kissed her.

Epilogue

Evie's heart swelled as she helped her sister set Callie's hair with gold-wire pins accented with silk bluebonnets hand-stitched by Aunt Martha. When Evie had suggested silver barrettes found online, Monte had strongly opposed the idea. As he hadn't voiced much of an opinion during their wedding planning, she'd happily conceded. She hadn't discovered until that morning that his aunt had lovingly made the pieces—for her and the girls.

She still teared up, thinking about all the hours Martha had spent, crafting each piece. Knowing her, she'd probably prayed for her, Monte and the twins, as she did.

If only she were here to see how beautiful Callie and Luna looked, and how proudly they wore their cherished pins.

When they weren't giggling about some surprise they and their father had concocted.

They also insisted Evie allow them to lead her, blindfolded, to the trailer, where she and her bridesmaids were now getting ready. One of Monte's ranch hands and groomsmen drove her there on the ATV while her mom and sisters brought her gown, veil, makeup, snacks and anything else she might want.

This would be her most memorable Christmas ever, by far.

Ms. Lucy, a woman Evie had come to love as much as

Monte and the girls did, entered the trailer, looked at her and pressed a hand to her chest. "Oh, my. Aren't you a vision?"

Wearing a silver-beaded lavender dress and blazer, she approached with outstretched arms and enveloped Evie in a hug. "That man of yours is liable to about lose his mind and his words, once he catches a glimpse of you." She glanced at Luna and Callie, for once looking identical from the top of their heads to their shoes. "And those precious munchkins of his. Still can't believe y'all got Callie to get dolled up without any fuss. Or that you let them plan the decorations."

Evie smiled. "I think it's wonderful he involved them."

"Some gals may worry about childish results."

"Is that a clue?" Lucy had to have seen the area on her way to the trailer and had probably paused to view it more thoroughly. "Because I'm pretty sure that's breaking the rules."

Monte had made it clear that anyone who stepped foot on the property was not to ruin his surprise.

"You aren't concerned at all?" Her sister's eyes held a teasing glint.

Evie shook her head. "I'm thrilled to see their creativity emerge. And am deeply touched by the gesture." This was also a great way for Monte to ensure the girls felt included and valued.

Ms. Lucy took Evie's hands in hers. "That, my dear, is one of the many reasons Monte adores you. And why Martha did as well."

Her heart squeezed as she thought about the woman responsible for her coming to the ranch.

"You have no idea how much joy it gave her to know this day was coming," she said.

Evie's laugh deepened with emotion. "Actually, I do. She told us often."

Ms. Lucy gave one quick nod. "That sounds like her. Watching out for her loved ones, right to the end."

She had, in so many ways. "I'm so glad I got to know her. To love her."

Ms. Lucy softly patted Evie's cheek. "Let this be her legacy."

She liked thinking of it that way, and of course, Ms. Lucy was right. While Martha hadn't raised Monte, she'd certainly influenced the man he'd become. She'd positively affected Evie as well, in so many ways.

For that, Evie would be eternally grateful.

It felt good to know Monte's community had welcomed her as their own. To think, when she first arrived at Sage Creek, she'd felt as if her boss had sent her to one of the worst locations ever. She now knew that assignment had been a gift sent from God—one that led to the best treasure of all.

Someone knocked on the door. Her mom answered to find Evie's father on the other side. Upon seeing Evie, his face sobered, and his eyes moistened. "Wow, darling. Just wow." He maneuvered around the others crammed in the tiny space and pulled her into a long, firm hug. Then he pulled away. "You too old for me to count those sun kisses?" He tapped her nose. "One. Two. Three."

She laughed, a lump lodged in her throat. "I love you."

"And I adore you. Your fiancé, too. That's saying a lot, considering we both recognize that no one, no matter how amazing, will ever be good enough for my little girl. Except maybe Monte Bowman."

"I'm glad you approve." Her joking tone didn't negate the truth in her words. As much as it meant that Monte's—and Martha's—people approved of her, she craved her father's blessing even more.

"All I've ever wanted is for you to be happy."

She kissed his cheek. "I know."

Whether it was her words or the moment, she wasn't sure, but he looked as if his emotions were about ready to overtake him.

He took a deep breath and straightened, donning the tense expression she'd seen him wear countless times when trying to regain composure. "You know, your mother and I were concerned when you insisted on a Christmas wedding."

"I could tell."

"Your mom was quite relieved to discover you were right about hill country winters being so much warmer than our Grand Rapids ones." Clearing his throat, he glanced about. "Line up, everyone. The groomsmen are waiting outside."

Her mom fanned a hand in front of her face and stepped forward. "I almost forgot." In her palm, she held four satin roses attached to safety pins. "Something used." She fastened them to the embellished band of Evie's Juliet cap veil. "My mother-in-law gave these to me shortly before your father's and my wedding. Stitched by her mother."

"They're perfect." They fit so well with the design she'd chosen, one couldn't tell they were an addition. That felt like a God-thing, as had so many other unexpected blessings leading up to this day. She didn't doubt that Aunt Martha's steady prayers in the months before her death played a part in that.

Evie never would forget the depth of the woman's faith.

Her mom grabbed a wooden box from the window ledge and opened it. "And something blue."

Inside lay three envelopes. The first bore her name in Aunt Martha's beautiful cursive writing. She'd made the next two out for the twins.

Tears blurred her vision as she opened her handcrafted card to reveal dried, pressed bluebonnets and the words, "Today you and Monte will experience a taste of heaven, revealed in a love pure and sweet. Enjoy the ceremony, dear. Dance, laugh, sing and know I'll be waiting for the day you all join me for the party that'll never end."

Her mom handed her a tissue, and gave her a squeeze. "That Martha was some woman."

Evie nodded. "The best."

Her mom turned to her husband. "You ready for this, Mr. Bell?"

He looked at Evie, moisture pooling in his eyes once again. "Don't ask me that now, my dear. Otherwise, I may become a blubbering idiot on our daughter's special day."

"I'm sure your baby girl won't mind in the least." Her mom smiled, kissed his cheek, then exited the trailer to meet the groomsman escorting her.

Evie squeezed into the narrow space leading from the bed to the entrance to form a line behind her. The soft notes of a harp soon followed, and the women exited one by one, leaving Evie with her dad, her sister and maid of honor, and the twins.

Holding her train aside, she lowered to the girls' eye level. "Thank you both for agreeing to do this important job."

Clutching their baskets filled with the tops of red silk rose petals dusted with white glitter, they stood a bit taller and nodded, expressions solemn.

They were so precious!

"We drop one with every step, right?" Luna began marching lightly in place, as if practicing.

"Exactly." While she wasn't that concerned with frequency, she knew they'd feel most comfortable with clear instructions. Not to mention, everyone would find their careful precision adorable.

Her sister stepped around her, poked her head out the door, then held it open. "All right, kiddos, you're up."

Callie squealed. Luna blanched and seemed frozen in place.

Evie placed a hand on her shoulder. "Deep breath."

The child complied.

Evie smiled. "You've got this. And I'll be right behind you."

Although Luna didn't seem convinced, she followed her sister out of the trailer.

The music shifted to country. She didn't remember Monte mentioning anything about that, or discussing songs at all.

Brow furrowed, Evie looked at her sister.

She beamed back at her. "Ready to get blown away?"

A jittery sensation swept through her. "I am." This was really happening. "So long as my legs don't turn to jelly, I'll be fine."

Her father took her hand and placed it in the crook of his arm. "You can lean on me." He released her to descend the metal stairs before her, then helped her down.

She turned the corner and gasped, tears immediately blurring her vision. Monte and the girls had placed at least a hundred poinsettias around the base of the gazebo. Twinkle lights glimmered from within the gold tulle draped from the top and around its support beams.

Beyond this stood numerous glass cylinders—more than she could count—filled with small white, gold and silver balls that glimmered in the sun.

Oh, Monte.

She was certain this day couldn't get any better.

But then Monte began to sing, his voice low and smooth.

She wobbled, and the tears she'd been fighting to contain spilled out.

Her dad placed an arm around her waist and gave her a squeeze. "This is what assured me that I was placing my daughter in the best possible hands."

"You knew?"

He nodded.

She loved knowing Monte had confided in her dad. She expected they'd become great friends.

Father, You're giving me blessings upon blessings.

A man she couldn't wait to spend the rest of her life with. Two precious daughters she loved as if they were her own. A town full of people who had done so much to help them this past year, during Martha's last few months especially. And her parents—her entire family, really—unreservedly fond of her soon-to-be husband.

It was almost more than her heart could take in.

Monte's voice caught watching his bride walk toward him wearing that same sweet blush that had stolen his heart the first day she arrived—and every day after. That woman had no idea how beautiful she was, which made her so stunning. Her loveliness extended well beyond her soft smile, wavy hair and silver-blue eyes.

His throat felt scratchy as intense emotions swept over him, but he kept singing. He'd painstakingly wrestled out every line in an attempt to convey, through lyrics, a love deeper than words could explain.

By God's grace, coupled with his umpteen hours of practice, he timed the last line with her last step. He handed Travis his guitar and faced the woman he'd be thanking Jesus for until his dying breath.

"Monte, I—I don't know what to say."

"I think the words you're looking for are, 'I do.'" He smiled, knowing if he didn't lighten the mood, he might not make it through the rest of the ceremony.

She and their guests laughed.

"Um." Holding the Bible to his chest, Pastor Roger shifted. "Y'all mind if I lead you through your vows before you go traipsing off into the sunset?"

More snickers from the people.

Monte nodded. "I'd like that very much."

The man who'd baptized him as a teen, counseled him when his ex-wife left, comforted them all when Aunt Martha passed, and officiated over the funeral, read a short passage on a love that always hopes, always fights and never ends. Then, he led them through the traditional promises Monte intended to keep—and exceed.

Pastor Roger grinned. "Then, by the power vested in me, I pronounce you husband and wife. Monte Bowman, you may kiss the bride."

He didn't need the prompt, because he'd already pulled her to him, knowing he would never let her go—figuratively. And in that moment, he wasn't sure he'd have the strength to release her physically, either.

He certainly wasn't in a hurry to do so.

Evie pulled away first. "I love you, Mr. Monte Bowman."

"And I love you, Mrs. Evie Bowman." He grinned. "Man, do I love the sound of that. Mrs. Bowman."

His girls, who'd been sitting *somewhat* patiently with his mom, ran up to him, pulling the bluebonnets from their hair. "Can we bring our flowers to Aunt Martha now?"

A lump lodged in Monte's throat as he surveyed the poinsettias, splashing the landscape with vibrant red. His aunt had planted their seeds the previous October, shortly before her death. Then, they'd housed the sprouting pots at Lucy's to keep Evie from discovering their plans.

The entire process had led to such joyful, anticipatory conversations between Aunt Martha, the girls and him. It had also allowed her to be a part of a special day that would never have come, if not for her.

They'd also created numerous priceless memories helping his aunt finish nearly half of her bucket list. When he expressed disappointment that they hadn't gotten to it all, she'd smiled and assured him they'd done more than she'd imagined, and that each excursion felt extra special because they'd all been together.

"Daddy?" Callie tugged on his arm. "Come *on!*"

He laughed. "Give us a minute to see to our guests."

Lucy stepped to his side. "You go. I'll direct everyone to the house for refreshments."

He smiled, grateful to retain yet another reminder of his aunt through his ongoing connection with her many friends. "I appreciate that."

He lifted Luna on his shoulders, twined his fingers with Evie as she reached for Callie, and walked toward his truck parked near the stables.

The mood felt hushed, sacred, on the drive into town, and even Callie spoke little as they made their way to his aunt's gravesite. But then, he handed them each an envelope. They were identical to the one his aunt had placed their cards in, only filled with dried bluebonnet petals.

Evie looked at him. "Did you know?"

"About what Aunt Martha made for you girls?" He nodded. "Decided to make the twins something similar, so they'd have something to give back to her." He knelt in front of his daughters and placed a hand on each of their shoulders, all of them encased in a solemn silence.

But then, as they deposited their flowers, one by one, on and around the gravestone, Luna began to sing softly. She was so quiet he almost didn't hear her, but then Callie joined in.

Tears pricked Monte's eyes as he thought back to that first spring, the despair he'd felt when his ex-wife had left him and the girls. His aunt had brought such joy when she arrived.

And with Evie by his side, he would experience joy for decades to come, much thanks to his aunt.

He'd probably never stop grieving the loss of someone so precious. But he also would be eternally grateful that God had brought something beautiful from it—a love so pure, so intense he still lost his breath whenever he held Evie Bowman in his arms.

* * * * *

Dear Reader,

In 2023, my beloved father-in-law passed away from cancer. God blessed us — his family—with an opportunity to share some of our favorite memories with him before he died, to tell him goodbye, and to pray with him. It was a precious time honoring a life lived well by a man who loved well.

In his last few days, I was able to witness the tenderness displayed to him by his hospice nurses, and I reflected upon what a holy and sacred—and painful—job they had. As they were working to ensure my father-in-law was as comfortable as possible, they assured my mother-in-law that she could call them at any time, day or night. I have no doubt that helped ease the burden my mother-in-law was carrying. I also have a strong feeling that, had she called late at night, she likely would've found them praying for her husband.

As I reflected upon John Slattery's life, and listened to the numerous stories shared by those who came to honor him after he passed, I was struck by the impact one person can have on numerous lives for generations. I saw that with my father-in-law, and also in Aunt Martha. I'm reminded of the verse that tells us, when all else fades, love, faith and hope will remain.

Thank you,
Jennifer

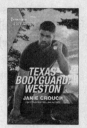